First Command

First Command

WILL COOK

Sagebrush
Large Print Westerns

Library of Congress Cataloging-in-Publication Data

Cook, Will..
 First command/ Will Cook.
        p.   cm.
ISBN 1-57490-463-9 (alk. Paper)
1. Soldiers—Fiction. 2. Large type books. I. Title.

PS3553.O5547 F57 2003
813'.54—dc21   2002153834

Cataloging in Publication Data is available from
the British Library and the National Library of Australia.

Sagebrush Large Print Westerns are published in the United
States and Canada by Thomas T. Beeler, Publisher, PO Box 659,
Hampton Falls, New Hampshire 03844-0659. ISBN 1-57490-463-9

Published in the United Kingdom, Eire, and the Republic of
South Africa by Isis Publishing Ltd, 7 Centremead, Osney
Mead, Oxford OX2 0ES England. ISBN 0-7531-6910-X.

Published in Australia and New Zealand by Bolinda Publishing
Pty Ltd, 17 Mohr Street, Tullamarine, Victoria, Australia, 3043
ISBN 1-74030-917-0

Manufactured by Sheridan Books in Chelsea, Michigan.

First Command

1

THIS WAS LIEUTENANT JEFFERSON TRAVIS' THIRD jolting day on the westbound stage and he was weary of traveling, weary of the dust and the oppressive heat and the miserable food served at the way stations. He was also disgusted with the company in which he traveled, two elderly officers, both first lieutenants at an age when they should have been majors. This told Jefferson Travis all he wanted to know about them: they were careless in their personal habits, lax in their duty, and now soured because promotion had passed them by. One was a quartermaster's assistant and the other a contract surgeon returning from leave. Since Travis was a cavalry officer, his commission barely ninety days old, he felt that he had no common thread of conversation to weave with these men.

A merciless sun beat down on the coach, and inside the temperature was a stifling hundred degrees, yet the leather curtains were drawn on the windward side to keep out the thick dust raised by the wheels. As far as Travis was concerned, this was a useless precaution. His uniform was unduly hot, for it was new and the sizing had yet to be laundered out. His tight-fitting collar, layered with abrasive dust, rubbed his neck raw, and his kepi, squared almost to the edge of his eyebrows, trapped sweat and allowed it to trickle down his temples, making runnels in his dust powdered cheeks.

The contract surgeon and the quartermaster's assistant sat in their shirtsleeves, unshaven, collars open; and now and then they drank from a common bottle. At first Travis hoped they would not offer him a

1

drink, then he hoped they would, so he might remind them of certain rules of deportment dealing with an officer drinking on a public conveyance.

He told himself that the heat was making him peckish, but he knew that wasn't all of it. Behind him were years of hard study; his commission hadn't come easily, and he was proud of his achievement, but no one else seemed to be. His father, even at the train, had gone on calling him "son," and the conductor, all the way to St. Louis had called him "young fella." Then when he got on the stage at Dodge City, the contract surgeon had said, "You can have that seat all to yourself, sonny."

Those were the only words said to him.

Jefferson Travis was twenty, but unfortunately he did not show his age. He was lanky, not yet filled out, and his hair was blond and fine, so that his beard, what there was of it, was little more than a lint on his chin and upper lip. He sat on the slick horsehair seat, arms outstretched, hands braced against the window frames to keep from sliding about. Some of his luggage lay between his feet; the rest was lashed on top.

The contract surgeon produced cigars and they lit them, adding an acrid bite to the dust swirling about the coach. They didn't offer one to Travis and he hadn't expected they would; they probably thought he was too young to smoke.

His saber lay beside him on the seat, and he kept the scabbard under his thigh to keep it from falling to the floor. Not a very good saber, but it was a gift from his father and the best he could afford, for he was a workingman whose wages had never been high. The pistol he wore had been bought in a New York moneylender's shop, a used .44 Smith & Wesson American, and Travis considered it a bargain at sixteen

2

dollars. The two officers across from him wore no weapons and somehow this pleased him; they were non-tactical, while he wore the cavalry yellow along his trouser leg and in the bandanna around his neck.

For the past hour he had been turning conversational openers over in his mind, such as: "Are you stationed at Fort Winthrop?" "This is my first tour of duty; I hope we become friends." "I haven't seen any Indians; they must be quiet this year."

He rejected the first as too ridiculous; of course they were going to Fort Winthrop, or else why would they be on the stage. The second was obvious; anyone who looked at him put him down as being fresh off the drill field. And the last was just plain stupid; he had never seen an Indian and wouldn't know a quiet one if he saw one.

Lieutenant Jefferson Travis was not a man overly impressed with himself; he knew that he didn't know much, but what he knew had been well learned. He supposed this was from growing up poor and hustling for everything that came your way. It wasn't a painful memory to recall that several winters he had spent his afternoons along the railroad tracks with a bucket of rocks, and when a train came by, he'd pelt the locomotive and the firemen would get mad and throw coal back. He'd pick this up, carry it home, and enjoy a warm house that night.

In school, when the knees of his pants were threadbare, he'd get the best marks, and then it didn't matter how poor you were; you were smart and polite and people liked smart, polite people. And later, when he discovered the charming company of girls, he had developed a ready wit to amuse them; it cost a lot less than taking them to the nickelodeon or to an ice cream

3

parlor.

But he was not at his best with strangers, and he wasn't much of a conversational opener. His forte was to wait and then comment; to let others act, then react. In his youth, and during the years at the Academy, he had brushed against a relatively unkind, unforgiving world without losing his sensitivity or his humor, and some of the time he thought he knew what he was doing, and part of the time he was sure, and with what remained he neither cared nor worried.

Yet he disliked being shut out of anything; he was a man who liked to participate, in a joke, a fight, anything. But there wasn't an opening here, and he didn't know how to make one for himself.

So he sat in stony silence and endured the miles that rumbled away beneath the iron-shod wheels.

In mid-afternoon the driver of the stage shouted and the contract surgeon put his head out the window and yelled jubilantly at a rider who was bearing rapidly down on them. The quartermaster's assistant crowded against the surgeon so he too could see. Then the rider pulled alongside and without breaking strides yelled, "How was Chicago, lieutenant?"

"Damned good! Climb aboard; I'll tell you about it!"

Travis then observed a credible feat of horsemanship, for the rider, a grizzled cavalry sergeant, left his saddle and jumped to the rocking coach without missing his grip or releasing the horse's reins: The door was opened and he came in, then tied his horse so that it could run alongside.

His glance touched Travis briefly, and he said, "If you move your feet there, son, I'll be able to get by." He sat down then and ignored Travis. "Case, you didn't get married in Chicago, did you?"

"Hell no," the surgeon said. "But she sure treated me like we were." He gleefully pounded a cloud of dust from the sergeant's shoulders, then offered him the bottle.

The sergeant upended it, swallowed heavily, smacked his lips and handed it back. "My, that's good. Cheap, but good." He glanced at Lieutenant Jefferson Travis' saber. "Do you find it necessary to take all the seat?" He wiped sweat from his face. "Your first tour of duty, huh? Well, I'll give you six months. Seen a lot of 'em come out, and a lot go back."

"I don't intend to go back, sergeant," Travis said.

"That's what most of them say, but they either resign or get a transfer." He looked at the two officers across from Travis. "I'll see you at Fort Winthrop." He opened the door and stood half in, half out.

The quartermaster officer said, "Take the bottle, Ben. You're welcome to it."

He laughed. "I'm closer to a full one than you are. Thanks anyway." He looked again at Travis and smiled, then made the saddle in one dangerous jump. A moment later he pulled ahead and was out of their line of vision.

"Who was that?" Jefferson Travis asked; he didn't care which one of them answered.

The contract surgeon said, "The best damned sergeant in the army. And the toughest, sonny. And he was being real generous when he gave you six months. But if you get to soldier with him, count yourself lucky."

On the frontier, where a soldier's year was recalled as a procession of monotonous days, it took but little to elevate one post above another, and Fort Winthrop's only real claim to this distinction was the river; the back gate was only a pistol shot from it, which meant that

5

even a buck private got his bath every Saturday night. One lonely road cut across the prairie in two directions, and each Wednesday a stage came through, using the fort as a relay station, and in exchange for this service the line carried dispatches to the far towns where details from Fort Winthrop established military order.

The fort's buildings and the encircling walls were adobe; there was nothing on the flat land to tease the eye except stunted sage and short grass and the limp scrub cottonwoods along the river. When it rained, the earth turned to gumbo mud, which then dried quickly and assumed the characteristics of iron; there was little change in between, for an hour after a rain the ground was already drying from a relentless sun. If there was one thing that Fort Winthrop had plenty of it was wind; it whistled in from the south, carrying the tantalizing flavors of the gulf waters as well as pecks of sand that sifted under collars and into the food. The sun also touched Fort Winthrop each day, very early in the morning, and by eleven o'clock a trooper could lay out a shovel and fry an egg on it thirty minutes later. This would have made field cooking quite simple, if they had ever had eggs along to fry.

Normally, the fort held three companies of cavalry, one company of infantry, a quartermaster detail of seventy men, and a substantial hospital staff. Time, circumstance, and a feeble appropriation from Washington had reduced this force to thirty-six men, nineteen of whom were non-tactical. The remainder were scattered along the north Texas-Indian Territory border in piddling outposts, and concerned with keeping the reservation-bound Indians in one place and the buffalo hunters from intruding, and the settlers from antagonizing both.

6

The government had a strong interest in this part of the country, for by putting the Indians on reservation they could not only make some effort to wean them from warlike habits, but also keep an eye on them so that settlers could move in. But this was accomplished at great expense, for agents and agencies had to be established and maintained and the Indians had to be fed; they were quick to understand the advantages of free handouts.

Yet in spite of its barren surroundings, the fort was a landmark and once every three months Sergeant Ben Arness saw it as he made his journey from Spanish Spring, sixty-odd miles to the northeast. Sixty miles of unchanging flats, buffalo wallows and dust and hell-heat in the summer, yet Arness always rode it in one fell swoop, stopping only twice, at the twenty- and forty-mile stage relay stations to change lathered horses. There was no reason for him to make this ride in such rapid fashion except that some men had to do things bang-rattle-clatter, and Arness was such a man. Some who knew him said he didn't care about anything, but he did. Some said he was born reckless, but that wasn't true; time and times had made him so. He always arrived near sundown, and as soon as he was admitted through the main gate, he rode directly to the stable.

He flung off there, then staggered to the watering trough while a stable private ran up with a bucket. Arness filled this, then slowly poured it over his head, letting it rinse away the grime and the ache of so much traveling. Then he climbed onto the low stable roof and stood there looking out on the eye-aching sweep of land as though he found it hard to believe he had come so far so fast. The sun was burning in a wood-smoke haze against the far horizon, turning it an orange-red with a hint of deeper purple. Every grass shadow was long and brush clumps appeared larger then normal, dark and thorny and spare-limbed. Grayness seemed to rise from the land, building darkness like an early morning tule fog builds a cloud, and when the sun was only a faint orange smudge below the earth, Arness came down the ladder to the ground.

The stable sergeant came over, rubbing his round, first-in-the-chow-line stomach. "What was your time this trip, Ben?"

"Nine hours and—" He paused to consult a large key-winder watch, "—forty-one minutes."

"I don't think you'll ever do it in nine hours flat," the sergeant said, as though he considered it a beastly shame. "Ben, how come you never count the time at the gate? It's always after you come down from the roof."

"The look is part of the ride I miss," Arness said. "You ever watch a sunset, Gurney?"

"Mess call at that time," the sergeant said, and went back into the stable working a toothpick between his teeth.

"I guess there's something in this world for everybody," Arness said half to himself. He took off his cavalry yellow neckerchief, and then his shirt, and wrung both dry before putting them on again. He was a stumpy man, about five-foot eight or nine, with short legs and arms like oak boles. His age was thirty-seven, yet he looked older, for his hair was graying and lines made a cracked mud mottle of his weathered skin. At seventeen he had stood in an Iowa cornfield and watched a squad of soldiers march by and the feeling had taken hold of him all of a sudden. He had left the plow standing there and with bare feet padding the spring earth, he had followed them and signed his name

8

before the recruiting officer. Of course his father had come after him, but it was too late; he had a contract to fulfill with the United States Army, and later Arness decided his father hadn't minded him joining. It was just that he hated to lose an able-bodied farm hand. In the years that followed there were many places to go, and he went, fought when he had to, and somehow survived it all. During the Civil War he made corporal, and afterward, he thought about getting out, but the army was pretty well rubbed into him by then and after eighteen years he got his sergeant's hooks.

He was a man of rugged competence, blocky-faced, blunt-mannered and without a blemish on his record; not one day of guardhouse time chalked up against him. Ben Arness did his job and waited, secure in the knowledge that promotion was slow and that a lot of officers were crowding fifty before they made captain, so he could wait for that last grade that would make him a sergeant-major, a top soldier.

Dusted, hair wetted down, he straightened his hat and neckerchief and walked across the parade ground, stamping his feet to ease the burning cramps of a saddle-borne sixty miles. His heels rattled the loose boards on the headquarters porch and he went into the orderly room.

"Sergeant Arness reporting," he said. "If you'll tell the major I'm here—"

"I think he's about ready to go to mess," the corporal said.

Arness' voice rose to a parade-field bellow. "If you'll tell the major I've ridden sixty miles without my supper—"

An inner door banged open and Major Deacon snapped, "Shut up that ox-calling and get in here!"

Arness whipped off his hat and clicked his heels as he came to attention; then he went in. "Close the damned door," Deacon said. "Sit down." He pushed a chair away from his desk and offered Arness a drink of whiskey and a good cigar, in that order. "Sergeant, just once couldn't you arrive, say, before mess, or a little after it?"

With the whiskey building a warm fire in his stomach, and the cigar fragrant between his teeth, Ben Arness found a smile. "You're the best officer I've ever served under, major."

"Now don't start buttering me up," Deacon said. He was a very tall man, and very thin, looking as though he had never fully recovered from some wasting illness. "Let's go out on the porch. The westbound stage is due in."

"I know. I caught up with it. Pickering and Case are on it. And a new lieutenant."

Deacon smiled. "That's your new lieutenant, and I don't want to hear any arguments about it."

Ben Arness groaned. "Aw, sir, did you have to?"

"Now you know someone has to take these new officers in hand and teach them the army. Here, put a few of these cigars in your pocket."

Arness grinned. "As long as you're bribing me, major, couldn't I take that bottle of whiskey too?"

A guard signaled that the stage was approaching and they went out to stand on the porch. It came rattling and careening across the flats and bucketed through the main gate, sawing to a rocking halt by the flagpole. The officer of the day stood by with a lantern as the passengers got down. Pickering went to his quarters and Case walked to the infirmary. Lieutenant Travis took a handkerchief from his pocket and wiped the grime from his shoulder boards.

Deacon, watching this, said, "If you say a word, Ben, you'll never see that bottle."

"Now, I wouldn't say anything, sir."

"You can even quit thinking it." The officer of the day came over and Deacon said, "Bring that new officer to my office. Come on, sergeant."

They went inside again and Deacon took his seat. A moment later a slightly hesitant step sounded in the orderly room; then Lieutenant Travis knocked, although the door was open.

"Come in," Deacon said.

Travis came to attention, saluted, and introduced himself, and when Deacon gave him "at ease," he looked at Ben Arness, a flicker of recognition in his eyes.

"Did you find your full bottle, sergeant?"

"I will in time, sir," Arness said.

In the lamplight Deacon could see Travis clearly, a week of peach down on his chin and upper lip. Travis' uniform showed hard use; he had slept in it since St. Louis and he itched with Dodge City lice. Now he stood before his commanding officer with the full realization that he was making an untidy impression. Travis had a spare, rather angular face with a thin, sensitive mouth. His eyes were pale dabs of brightness in deep sockets.

"Please sit down, Mr. Travis," Deacon said. "I believe you met Sergeant Arness on the stage."

"He asked me to move my feet," Travis said pleasantly. "But we didn't exchange names."

Major Deacon cleared his throat and shuffled some papers on his desk. "Mr. Travis, I never coddle a new officer. The quicker he gets to his duty, the quicker he finds his place in the service. I'm sure Sergeant Arness

11

will agree with that."

"Yes, sir," Travis said. "I'm sure the sergeant would never disagree with the major."

Deacon frowned and his eyebrows drew together. "Did you two have words on the stage?" He glanced from Travis to Arness, then back again.

"It was a most pleasant conversation," Travis said, smiling. "Wouldn't you say so, sergeant?"

Arness squirmed a bit in his chair. "Yes, sir, most pleasant."

"Well," Deacon said, rubbing his hands together. "There's no reason why you can't go with Sergeant Arness in the morning then. Your luggage can accompany you by pack horse. I don't imagine you brought too much."

"No, sir, just a small trunk and a satchel." His glance touched Ben Arness again. "Not much to bring, not much to take with me when I go. Wouldn't you say that was right, sergeant?"

Arness frowned and studied his blunt fingers. "Whatever the lieutenant says, sir."

"What's going on here?" Deacon asked. "Who's leaving?"

Travis' expression was innocent. "No one, sir. I believe you were about to explain my duties."

"Yes, I was," Deacon said. Again his glance flicked from one to the other. Then he leaned back in his chair, resting one hand on the edge of his desk, his arm straight and still. "Your detail is billeted at Spanish Spring, a small town sixty miles northeast of here. North, across the river, is the Indian reservation. Of course some of it has been opened up to settlers, and farther north, the buffalo hunters make their yearly migrations with the herds. Mr. Travis, I'm not going to

12

lie and tell you that your duty will be easy. The situation there is peculiar, but I suppose we are living in peculiar times. Recruitments are down and the frontier posts are at less than a quarter strength, with no hope of getting more men in the immediate future. Of course, officers in Washington are trying to get us more money, but like it or not, the military is ultimately controlled by the civilians, the politicians who vote us the money on which we operate. However, we face a situation worse than no money or troops. The Department of Interior controls the Indians; they expect the army to help keep them on reservation. Yet the Interior Department is highly critical of military policy; they blame much of the Indian unrest on past military campaigns against Indians. You'll have to work with the Indian agent, but I'm afraid without much cooperation."

"I'm sure I'll manage diplomatically, sir."

"Yes," Deacon said doubtfully. "There's something else too, Mr. Travis. Strong political forces in Washington feel that the Indians have no right to the land, and have pushed through legislation authorizing settlers to farm certain choice sections of the reservation. Needless to say, the Interior Department is unhappy, the Indian Agent is unhappy, and the Indians are making war talk. You will, of course, assume the responsibility for the settlers' safety, but be sure not to antagonize the Indian agent when you do it."

"I believe I understand," Jefferson Travis said dryly. "Sort of like grabbing oneself by the nape of the neck and holding oneself out at arm's length."

"Well, I wouldn't put it quite that way," Deacon said. "There is a third matter that needs airing, Mr. Travis. Colonel Dodge has been largely instrumental in opening the plains country; Dodge City, new and brawling as it

13

is, bears his name, and he has considerable influence in Washington. Colonel Dodge feels that the Indians *and* the settlers ought to get the hell out and leave the country open to the buffalo hunters. He has, in some way, made it an army responsibility to see that there is no trouble between settlers, Indians, and his buffalo hunters. Dodge City is their headquarters, you know."

"Yes, I passed through there," Travis said. He wiped his thin lips with his fingers. "Let me see if I have this straight, sir. The Indians hate the army, the settlers, and the buffalo hunters. And the settlers hate the army, the Indians, and the buffalo hunters. Of course it stands to reason that the buffalo hunters hate the Indians and the settlers." His face was perfectly straight.

The major threw Travis an oblique glance, not quite sure of what was happening.

"It's not as impossible as it sounds," Deacon said uneasily. "Army policy is to maintain a reasonable vigilance. I just don't want to forward reports that will force my superiors to battle political factions. Conduct a one-eye-open policy, Mr. Travis."

"Wouldn't you say, sir, that it was more of a both-eyes-closed policy?" His amused eyes touched Ben Arness. "I'm sure you agree with me, sergeant."

"The matter is not for debate," Deacon said flatly, sure now that he was being gently ribbed. "We do the best we can, Mr. Travis. And don't call for additional troops; I don't have a man to spare. Given some trouble right now, I couldn't muster enough men to load the quartermaster wagons."

"Do you mean, sir, that I have only one company of cavalry at Spanish Spring?"

Deacon stared at him. "One company, hell! You have fourteen men." He tapped his fingers on his desk and

14

pursed his thin lips. "Mr. Travis, you have a very honest face. I'm going to be quite truthful with you. Sergeant Arness has been at Spanish Spring three years, and in that time, two junior officers have requested relief from their duty and reassignment."

"Because of the duty or Sergeant Arness, sir?"

"Ah, so you did have words on the stage!" He shook his bony finger at each of them. "You two are going to get along, is that understood? Mr. Travis is not going to get a transfer, and you, Ben, are going to behave yourself." This seemed to settle the matter as far as Deacon was concerned. "Now I imagine you'd like a bath and a clean bed, Mr. Travis. Just take any empty quarters you find across the parade; the officers' picket row is nearly vacant, that's how far under strength I am."

"Thank you," Travis said, rising. "I'd like to see you before tattoo, sergeant."

"Yes, sir," Arness said glumly. After Travis went out, Arness helped himself to another of Deacon's cigars. "Why did you assign him to me, sir?"

"Now he's a nice boy, you can see that. Give him a chance, Ben."

"He's not army," Arness said sourly. "His father wasn't army either. You can tell, sir, just by looking at 'em. A second-hand pistol and a cheap saber, and you've got another civilian in uniform ready to put in a tour so he can resign his commission and get a soft job back East. I give him six months, sir."

"It's easier to get sergeants," Deacon said, "than Academy graduates. It may pay you to remember that. But I like him. Like the cut of him. At least he's got a sense of humor, even if he's so new he doesn't know the buckskin bottom of his breeches from an adobe brick."

15

He tipped his chair back and smiled gently. "In a way he reminds me of myself on my first assignment. My father was a schoolteacher, sergeant. He wanted me to be one too, and I don't think he ever forgave me for entering the Academy. So I know how Mr. Travis feels, without the 'proper' background. Every officer and twenty-year sergeant will try to break his back just to see if it's brittle. And if he survives it and is lucky enough to find a woman who can stand the life, he might have a son who'll find it easier, because he comes from an 'army family.' God damn it, Ben, the army isn't some kind of a religion, you know!"

"It is to me, sir," Arness said flatly. "It's my whole life; I'd rather die than retire." He puffed on the cigar a moment, then laughed. "I can get along with Mr. Travis, sir, because he won't last. He's still a kid, and he'll find out it isn't his kind of army; no parades and gay cotillions. And when he gets on that stage to go back East, I'll be watching him, because it *is* my kind of army."

Major Deacon studied Ben Arness carefully before speaking. "You're a hard, unbending man, Ben. A long time ago you made up your mind and nothing's going to change it. All right, so a good many Academy men resign after their first tour. What about the rest, men like me?" He saw that he wasn't going to change Arness' mind, so he waved his hand. "Go on, Ben, get out of here and let me eat a cold supper."

Arness always took a room in the bachelor officers' row, although it was not permitted by regulations; he seemed to find satisfaction in this sort of thing, as though he waged some constant war with the commissioned ranks, trying to establish himself on an equal basis with them.

16

He filled two water buckets for his bath, then undressed and got in the tub and scrubbed clean. Afterward he dressed in clean blues and went to find Lieutenant Travis, not that he wanted to, but because he knew a green second lieutenant could get a sergeant in as much trouble as a colonel.

Travis was not difficult to find; he was sitting on his bunk, dubbing his boots when Ben Arness stopped in the open doorway.

"Come in, sergeant. Sit down." He put dubbing and cloth aside. Then Arness took a chair, balancing his felt campaign hat on his knee. Travis studied Arness, trying to decide what to say; he knew he had to say something, even the wrong thing. "Sergeant, you've spent more time in the army than I have years in my life. But I don't think that entitles you to special privileges. No one came up to me and handed me this rank. I studied for it, and because I'm not the smartest man in the world, I had to study hard."

"Yes, sir."

"It's amazing how much disrespect you can get into a 'sir,' isn't it?" He smiled. "All right, sergeant, so we're not going to be friends. But I'll tell you one thing, we're both in the same army, and we'll work for the army. What was your reason for riding here?"

"To make a report to Major Deacon and pick up the payroll."

"I'll take charge of the payroll in the morning," Travis said. "What is it about me that rubs you so raw, sergeant? My age? Or the gold bars and the age combined?"

"Do you really want to know, sir?"

"I asked you, didn't I?"

"Let me ask you something, sir. What made you

17

choose the army?"

"Because it was a chance to get an education," Travis said. "An officer's folks do not necessarily have money, sergeant."

"Are you going to stay in the army, sir?"

"I don't know," Travis said frankly. "I'll know after I've been here awhile. Why? Does it matter to you?"

"Yes, sir, it does," Arness said. "It means I've got to put my life, and the lives of my men in a greenhorn's hands while you make up your mind whether you're going to soldier or just mark time."

"I see," Travis said softly. "What do you want? A man to be born an old soldier?" He picked up his key-winder watch and tightened the spring. "I'll expect to leave at six in the morning. Have the horses ready."

"Yes, sir," Arness said and went out, his footfalls heavy on the duckboards. Travis waited a moment, then blew out the lamp and settled in his bunk; a deep sense of depression dogging him.

2

BEFORE DAWN, LIEUTENANT TRAVIS BREAKFASTED alone, then gathered his luggage and carried it to the stable where Ben Arness was readying a pack horse. Arness nodded coolly and Travis didn't bother to speak; he felt no compulsion to carry on a conversation with this man.

While Arness went to the sutler's place, probably to get a bottle, Travis woke the paymaster and signed for the payroll he was to take for the Spanish Spring detail. He stowed this in his saddlebag and joined the sergeant by the flagpole in the center of the parade ground.

"You want to follow the stage road, sir?" Arness asked.

"Whichever is the shortest distance between the two points," Travis said. His voice had not yet attained the full manly resonance that he wanted. At the Academy he had practiced many hours before a mirror, trying to develop a commanding manner, but he could never quite bring it off. Some men were born with piercing eyes and a deep voice; he hadn't been. So he always chose his words carefully, hoping they were strong enough to carry the conviction his manner couldn't.

Be firm, be brief, be final; he tried to live by these edicts.

"Cross-country it is then," Arness said and stepped into the saddle.

A four-man detail came on the post, tired from an all-night search for two lost horses. Travis and Arness passed this detail while going through the main gate, just as the sun began to blush redly on the horizon;

19

Travis rode a few feet behind Arness, letting him establish the direction and pace. The sun didn't take long to get hot. By nine o'clock they were both sweating and squinting, and at eleven the heat bounced a shimmer off the parched land and made their eyeballs ache from the glare of it. They rode in an endless sea of stunted grass and withered brush, a land of unspeakable monotony, unbelievably barren. Far to the north a smudge marked some low buildings and Lieutenant Travis said, "Is that a shack, sergeant?"

"A shack and a waterhole. Somebody's trying to ranch a little."

"You're joking," Travis said. "Sergeant, a jack rabbit couldn't subsist out here."

"Well, people try anyway, sir. A man can make it if he learns to eat out of a scoop shovel and live in a hole in the ground." He waved his hand in the direction they were traveling. "They come and go, sir, just like second lieutenants. Some leave a mark on the earth, and some don't." He looked at Travis, a flat speculation in his eyes, as though he waited to see whether or not he was going to get away with this. But he knew he would. They were alone and he could say what he wanted to; there were no witnesses.

He wants me to argue with him, Travis thought. He wants me to steam a little and get mad at him and pull my rank on him so he can tell himself that he was right, that here is another second lieutenant who can't survive a man-to-man relationship but who has to hide behind his congressionally appointed rank.

"When I came through Kansas I sat for hours looking out the train window at the flatness of the land," Travis said. "Where are the hills, sergeant?"

"We got hills, not very high though." Then he looked

at Travis and grinned. "You want me to give you the fifty-cent tour, sir? I always give new lieutenants the fifty-cent tour. I answer all the questions, about Indians, the country, the buffalo, and what you ought to know about the army."

"I'm sure you're a gold mine of information," Travis said. "So when recruitment picks up, I'll see that you get a few men to impress."

Color came into Ben Arness' sun-darkened cheeks. "You don't insult very easy, do you, sir?"

"I'm sure I do, sergeant, but I've learned to ignore the complaints of the mentally retarded, immature children, and crotchety old sergeants. While you lull yourself into believing that you won't have to put up with me for very long, I rest secure, believing that you'll retire from active service and sit on some saloon porch and tell everyone how you ran the army."

Ben Arness quickly wheeled his horse around so that he faced Travis, who pulled his horse to a stop. They looked at each other, anger and open resentment in Arness' eyes, and a cool-headed watchfulness in Jefferson Travis'. Then Arness whipped off his hat and smashed it against his leg, and again turned his horse and resumed his pace, so angry that he could not speak.

Indistinct in the distance was another group of buildings, another settler trying to scratch out an existence. Travis and Arness rode toward it and later Travis looked back toward the other place they had seen, but it was blended into the heat-smeared horizon. Arness rode with his felt campaign hat tipped low over his eyes to shield them from the merciless sun.

"Rink's place," he said. "I never stop anymore. They're an unfriendly bunch."

"Let's stop this time," Travis said. He rather enjoyed

21

being contrary with Ben Arness. He watched Arness' mouth compress and the cheeks draw flat against the bones, and his neck go stiff while he stared fixedly ahead.

Travis could now see Rink's place quite clearly: a low sod house, a corral, and middling-sized barn. As they approached, two men came out of the soddy; they carried rifles. A woman eased past them, a hand to her forehead to shield her eyes. Then she turned and went back in while the two men came forward to meet Travis and Arness.

"Hidy," one said. He was a gaunt man, with a full mustache and dark eyes rather closely spaced. He wore knee-length boots, ragged-kneed jeans, and no shirt at all; his once red underwear was now a pale pink, grimy at the collar and worn through at the elbows.

These men were brothers; Travis could see the common whelping stamped on them. Ben Arness said, "This is Pete Rink. His brother, Oney."

"Hidy," the other one said.

"The woman is their wife," Arness said. "Name's Esther."

"*Their* wife?" Travis said.

"She be," Oney Rink said. "Pete and me shared the same breast as little yonkers. Somehow we never lost the habit of sharin'." He looked at Travis as though he expected him to make something out of it, because others had. "Wimmen is scarce out here. Esther's satisfied. So're we. If you don't like it, ride on. Got no use for the army anyway."

"Me neither," Pete Rink said.

They still carried their rifles, brass-receivered Henrys, and Travis wished they'd point them somewhere else. "You can put the rifles down," Travis said pleasantly.

"We don't intend you any harm."

"I sleep with my gun," Oney Rink said.

"Me too," Pete Rink said.

Travis looked at him, then at his brother. "Doesn't he ever say anything except 'me neither' and 'me too'?"

"Got an agreement," Oney Rink said. "I do the talkin', he does the listenin'. Never quarrel that way. If you got no more business here, I'd oblige you to get."

"Well, we'd be grateful to eat in the shade of your barn," Travis said. "If that isn't asking too much."

"Don't allow anyone near the barn," Oney stated flatly. "That includes army. I said my hidy, now I'll say goodbye."

Ben Arness was ready to let the whole thing go at that, but Jefferson Travis didn't want to. He'd met a few irascible people in his life, but the Rinks were a breed apart. He could understand that their stark existence on this land made them suspicious and mistrustful, but he felt that the army, like a policeman, was just something everyone should trust.

Travis stepped down from his horse and handed the reins to Ben Arness. "I'll fill the canteens from the seep, sergeant. You'd better get the horses in the shade." He looked at Oney Rink. "We're not going to hurt your barn, mister. It's just blasted hot in this sun."

"I said my say," Oney Rink declared. "I start shooting next."

Travis frowned and smiled at the same time. "What?" His voice was incredulous. Clearly he found this hard to believe.

"Be careful now," Ben Arness warned softly.

"I've had enough of this nonsense," Travis said flatly. "By golly, I'm going to have my rations in the shade!" He waved his hand at Arness and turned his back on the

23

Rinks. "Go fill the canteens, sergeant."

He turned toward the barn and took three steps when Ben Arness yelled, then a rifle went off with a sharp crack and Jefferson Travis felt a tug on his forearm heavy enough to spin him half around. He fell to one knee, his hand jerking at the leather holster flap.

Ben Arness jabbed spurs into his horse and rode Oney Rink down. The man screamed and thrashed on the ground, his hands clutching his crushed chest; then Travis was running back, his revolver in his hand. He jabbed the muzzle into Pete Rink's rib cage and said, "Drop it! God damn it, I said, drop that rifle!" This sudden flare of reasonless violence shocked him numb, but he forced himself to function, to maintain control of his emotions.

Arness was dismounting and the woman ran out of the soddy and stared at Oney Rink. She was of an indefinable age, young, but hard used by the country. Her body was round, but her breasts beneath her cotton sack dress were flat and formless. She stood there silent, brushing strands of hair from her homely face. Pete Rink did not move while Arness knelt by the dead man.

Blood ran down Travis' arm and into his glove, and he took it off and held it under his arm while he rolled his sleeve to examine the wound. The bullet had caught him below the elbow, in the muscle, and ripped out a respectable amount of flesh, making it ugly but not serious.

"Is he dead?" Travis asked, still trying to believe it had happened so suddenly.

"Yes, sir. When the horse reared, he caught him with both front hooves."

"Go take a look in that barn," Travis said. Voicing the command helped him to maintain his self-control.

24

Arness stood up, then looked at the blood dripping from Travis' fingers. "That serious, sir?"

"Just a pink. I've had worse in saber drill. Go on with it now."

Arness looked at Pete Rink for a moment, then trotted toward the barn. The woman scratched her breast and pushed nervously at her hair, still staring at the dead man.

"What's the matter with him?" Travis asked, nodding toward Pete Rink. "Doesn't he know he's dead?"

"I guess he's been told what to do for so long, he can't think or do for himself." She stepped away from Travis, then looked back at him. "Did you have to kill him, mister?" She didn't wait for his answer, but took Pete Rink by the arm and turned him toward the house. He wore the expression of a man who is hopelessly lost, and the woman patted his arm, speaking soft, soothing words to him. "He ain't all there in the head, mister." With this explanation, she led him away to the soddy.

Ben Arness came back from the barn, leading two horses. "Army," he said. "They didn't want us to see 'em, I guess." He took off his hat and then wiped his mouth with the back of his hand. "I guess they found the horses and figured to sell them for thirty-forty dollars apiece. It may be hard for you to understand, but the horses are more important to these people than the man who was killed over 'em. Eighty dollars, sir, would have fed them for a year and bought some seed, new clothes, and a jug of whiskey. That's a lot of comfort to people like them. Probably more'n they ever saw in their lives. They'd kill to get less than that." He looked at Travis' arm, still bleeding. "You ought to put something on that." He hesitated, then added, "I've got a bottle of whiskey." Clearly he implied that it was a rotten shame

25

to waste it on a thing like this, but he got it and uncorked it, then poured some on the wound. The young man's face went white and he caught his breath sharply. "Prance around a little, if it'll make you feel any better, sir."

"Thank you, sergeant. I believe I will." He stamped his feet in a small circle, waving his arm like he was trying to snap something sticky off the fingertips. Then he took off his neckerchief and wrapped it around the wound. "For a minute there, sergeant, we were on the same team. Any regrets?"

"Well, sir, I pitched in because I just didn't think I could explain to Major Deacon how I lost an officer five hours out of Fort Winthrop." He shook his head. "I told you to go easy, sir. People out here mean it when they say they're going to shoot." He blew out a breath of long duration. "I expect you want to take the damned horses along, huh?"

"They're army property, aren't they? Better see if you can find a shovel. We'll help with the burial." He turned then and walked into the soddy. Some packing crates had been fashioned into a table and two benches. An old cast-iron stove sat in one corner, and a brass double bed across the room. Buffalo chips were piled behind the stove, and litter lay around on the dirt floor where it had been flung.

The woman was brewing some chicory coffee, and Pete Rink sat at the table, staring at nothing. Suddenly he turned and looked at Jefferson Travis.

"I guess you're going to take the horses too," he said defeatedly. He spread his hands and laid them flat on the table. "Oney, he just meant to nick you a little, scare you off, that's all."

"We'll help you with the burial," Travis said. "I'm

26

really sorry it turned out this way."

"Nothin' turns out good for us," Pete Rink said softly. "And I'll bury him, mister. It's my place."

"Why don't you just go, like Oney asked, mister?" Esther asked. Her voice was curiously toneless and devoid of emotion. "Ain't it bad enough we got to lose without havin' someone watch us?"

"I'm very sorry," Jefferson Travis said and went out. Arness had found a rusty shovel, but he threw it aside when Travis stepped into the saddle. Arness fastened the lead ropes of the recovered horses to the pack horse, then gathered the reins of his own mount.

Pete Rink came out of the soddy and Arness left his horse and picked up the two rifles, levering the cartridges out of the magazines. He dropped these in his pocket and mounted; they turned silently out of the yard and when they were a few hundred yards out, Jefferson Travis turned his head and looked back. Pete Rink had taken off his brother's boots and was putting them on, and the sight of him, sitting there in the dust, trying to salvage something, hit Travis like a cold clod in the stomach.

"Don't they feel anything, sergeant?"

Arness looked at him, then shook his head. He reached into his pocket and brought out two cigars, offering one to Travis. "Here, sir, second lieutenants are old enough to smoke." He furnished the light, and after his was going, he said, "I seen kids die of the fever out here. I've seen their folks bury 'em in the morning, and go back to the plowin' an hour later. If they didn't, they'd be that much farther set back. You got to have *time* to cry, sir. Got to have time for grief. And they got no time at all. There's just so much luck in the world, sir. A man can't make it and he can't destroy it. Now

27

when a man comes into some luck, he ought to stop and think a minute, because someone else has just lost a little. These people, they've lost it all, sir. They lost it all so long ago that they don't know a bad thing when it happens, because what's bad to some is just normal for them." He pointed to the prairie ahead. "There's some buffalo wallows about a mile or so. We can eat there and rest the horses."

Travis had never seen a wallow, but as they neared one, he found that the prairie around it was littered with buffalo droppings. The wallow was a large depression in the earth, well trampled, with a dried mud bottom. They dismounted and broke out cold rations. Travis took off his kepi and placed a wet handkerchief over his head, then put the kepi back on to keep the sun off his neck.

"What causes these wallows, sergeant?"

"No one really knows," Arness said. "I guess it starts with a little hollow in the ground that collects water. The buffalo wallow around in it and make it a little deeper. After a hundred years, it gets like this." He took a long pull from his canteen. "Maybe it takes a thousand years. One's pretty much like the other out here."

"Or six months, sergeant?"

Ben Arness looked at him, then laughed. "You go pokin' your nose in people's barns, sir, and it won't be six months. No horses are worth it." Then he shrugged. "Well, you've got to write the report, I don't."

Travis regarded him solemnly. "What made you join the army, sergeant?"

"Because there was nothing for me on the outside," Arness said. "I was a farm boy, and it was poor land. Just a lot of hard work and nothing to look forward to. My father was fifty before the land became his. He'd have to die before I got it." His beefy shoulders rose and fell. "All I know is the army. Put me out and I wouldn't know where to go, what to do. But you wouldn't understand. It's not your life."

"What is my life then?"

Arness shook his head. "A tour here, probably, then resign. Then a good job someplace, where you can wear a clean shirt and celluloid collar and carry a cane. I've seen a hundred come and go, sir, and it's always as if they've taken something that's mine and used it and put some of it in their pocket so that I can't get it back."

"I see," Travis said softly. "And I really do see, sergeant. Any family?"

"No," Arness said. "Why?"

"I don't know. All this emptiness out here makes me think of home, and my family. My father's a bricklayer."

Arness frowned, and studied Travis. "Is that the truth? I never knew they'd take a bricklayer's kid into the Academy. Just a bricklayer, huh?"

"Just a bricklayer. He's never made more than ten dollars a week in his life." The sun dried out the handkerchief under his kepi, so he refreshed it from his canteen. "My brother, Paul, is a clerk in the barrel factory near my home. He makes fourteen dollars a week and someday he'll be manager." He leaned back until he was almost supine. "I chose the army, sergeant, just the way you did, and for quite possibly the same reasons. When I finished high school, I could have gone to work, maybe as a junior clerk in a law firm, or a brokerage house; my father wanted that. But I wanted to see something, a great big lot of something."

"Dust and scrub grass?"

"Well, that's *something,* isn't it? Sergeant, I stood on

29

a depot platform in Kansas and listened to a train whistle blow five miles away. Can you imagine that, five miles? That's how big and still it was. Back East it's so crowded and noisy such a thing would be impossible. And the life is so humdrum. You just go home every night on the same street and wear the same suit to church every Sunday." He chuckled softly. "And when I write home and tell them about all this, they aren't going to believe any of it."

Arness grunted, and then they were silent for a while. They mounted up and wore out the rest of the day at a walk, to save their animals, and that night they stopped for a fire and a hot meal, backfat and wheatcakes. Afterward they made coffee in the skillet and washed their tin plates in the dirt.

Travis' arm was paining him badly and he kept it against his stomach, his hand thrust into the waistband of his trousers. Thinking back about the things he had discussed with Arness, Travis wondered if his increased understanding of the man would allow them to work more amicably together. He hoped that this would be so, but he wondered about Ben Arness. The man was so entrenched in his ways that there was little hope of him changing.

They were resting, stretched out on the ground, and from the darkness, Ben Arness said, "The arm giving you hell, sir?"

"I'll get along with it," Travis said. "But I'd appreciate another cigar, if you have one."

Arness handed it over, then said quite frankly, "You're going to have to start buying your own."

After the cigar was ignited, Travis lay back again and looked at the sky. "That's the biggest, blackest sky I ever saw," he said. "And the brightest stars. It's easy to think that everyone's moved off the earth except yourself."

"I'll bet you wrote poetry to the girls," Arness said dryly.

"I did, sergeant, and it wasn't bad. You know, I've always had a flair for that sort of thing." Then he raised up and peered at Ben Arness. "Sergeant, you want to know something? You're not going to rile me. I'm going to see the day when you get blue in the face and run out of cuss words, and you're going to know then, sergeant, that you've been out-soldiered. Now you put that in your pipe and smoke it, and I'll lay money that it's no worse than these rope cigars."

"Some people have no gratitude," Arness said sourly.

3

AS HE RODE THROUGH THE DARKNESS WITH BEN
Arness, breathing the dust raised by the dull thud of the
horses' hooves and feeling it settle on his face, Jefferson
Travis reflected on how little one person really learned
about another through conversation. All you could glean
were surface impressions; you had to dig deep for the
truth. Arness had spoken of his youth on the farm, and
why he had left it, but Jefferson Travis knew that the
things that were left unsaid were often the more
important aspects of a man's life. He knew because this
was true of himself.

He had come from a genteel but very poor home, a
proper home, one full of virtue and free of disgrace,
except, of course, for Uncle Timothy, who drank. But
nobody mentioned this. Just as nobody admitted the
poorness of their circumstances. Jefferson as a boy had
quickly learned that he could do practically anything to
alleviate those circumstances, provided he did it
unobtrusively, and provided it hurt no one. So he
discovered the difference between hypocrisy and pride,
and he never forgot the hard lessons that respectable
penury taught. But there was a great longing in him to
shed pretense of any kind, and he knew he could never
do it at home. Indeed, although the Academy was a
revered institution, his people had felt betrayed when he
secured an appointment there and left their way of life.
It was as though he hadn't really approved of them and
wished to elevate himself out of their class. He hadn't
been able to explain his real reasons, that he wanted
only to become a man in his own right.

32

"There's lights ahead, sir," Arness said, snapping Travis away from his thoughts.

"Is that Spanish Spring?" He studied the faint sparkle of lights. The night was very clear with not a breath of wind stirring, but the lights winked like stationary fireflies.

"Yes, sir. About an hour now, sir."

In the cool of night it was difficult to recall how hot it had been during the day; Travis would have welcomed a jacket now. Had he been traveling alone, he would probably have stopped for the night and rolled into a blanket, but he had hesitated to suggest this lest Arness think him tender-bottomed.

They reached the edge of town and rode down the dark streets. It was a small town, laid out around the courthouse, an ugly, adobe building flanked by gnarled trees. The main street was a wide, dusty strip, bracketed by flat-fronted adobes, and only the saloon and hotel were still open.

The United States Cavalry detachment occupied what had once been a large trading post. It was surrounded by a low mud wall and the building was U-shaped, with a stable and wagon yard in back. They dismounted in front and Jefferson Travis stepped stiffly to the ground.

Ben Arness said, "The center part is an office, with mess and quarters on either end. The troopers' barracks is on the right, sir; we use the other wing for a storeroom."

"Take the horses around back, sergeant," Travis said. He turned and looked up and down the compound. "I don't see any guards."

"Well, sir, we haven't been posting any. With fourteen men, sir, it's every man to his duty, and the less extra he has to do—"

33

"I quite understand," Travis said. "We'll let it stay like that."

Arness was pleasantly surprised; he had been prepared to put up with guard duty and all the garrison foolishness that new officers liked so well. "Thank you, sir." He took the horses and led them around to the stables while Travis went inside.

He fumbled about until he found a lamp and put a match to it, adjusting the wick until the flame was bright, then he turned and surveyed the room with some distaste. There were a desk, a bookcase, four chairs and a brass spittoon, with some brightly colored Indian blankets adorning the walls. Dust and old papers lay about and this offended Travis' sense of order.

As soon as Sergeant Arness came back, Travis said, "Sergeant, is there a well nearby? Good! Fetch me about four pails of water, some soap, and a mop."

"You're going to scrub it out tonight?"

"I intend to open this office at reveille, sergeant, and I don't want anyone to mistake it for the stable." He stepped to an adjoining door and opened it; this was his quarters. Holding the lamp high, he looked at it critically and found it neat enough for occupancy. He turned back to Arness. "I asked for water, sergeant."

He worked until nearly daylight, scrubbing the floors, washing the windows, clearing out the rubbish and dust, and only a strong compulsion to do the job right kept him from lying down on his bunk and going to sleep.

Corporal Busik brought him his breakfast, and he met the rest of his detail afterward at roll call. Travis made no speech; they were all professional soldiers, with more guardhouse time than he had total time in the army. He tried to be crisp and to the point, merely stating that the army operated by rules, which he had

34

memorized, and they were expected to follow them.

Sergeant Arness, whose duty it was to relay an officer's commands, went into the office and stood while Travis sat down behind his desk.

"Who are the legally constituted authorities in this town, sergeant?"

"The sheriff, sir, Owen Gates. And a judge."

"Send for the sheriff. I want to report on the trouble at the Rink's place. It wouldn't do for the local powers to be able to say that the army didn't cooperate."

"I don't think the sheriff's up yet, sir."

"Well damn it, get him up!" He took out his watch and popped the lid on it. "I'm going to bathe and shave. Shall we say, thirty minutes, sergeant?"

"Yes, sir." He shifted his feet on the plank floor and cleared his throat. "Lieutenant, that matter at Rinks—ah, you ought to talk to General Wrigley about it. I've always taken him into my confidence, sir."

"Who in blazes is General Wrigley?"

"Well, sir, he's the president of The Dixie Land Development Company. Most of the settlers around here lease their land from the general, sir. When he hears about it, he'll come here anyway, and I guess it'd look better, sir, if you invited him."

"All right," Travis said.

Arness left and Travis took a pair of buckets around to the well for his bath water. He squatted in the tub as long as he dared, to soak some of the weariness out of his bones, then shaved carefully and brushed the dust from his uniform. He still hadn't found time to unpack his belongings; his satchel lay on his bunk, and the chest sat in one corner where he had shoved it with his foot.

While he waited, he looked out past the low walls at the town, now bathed in the bland early morning sunlight. Around in back, a detail of troopers curried the horses, and three others, under Corporal Busik's direction, diligently straightened out the storeroom, not knowing when the new officer would pull a surprise inspection.

Travis had written his first order and it was posted outside his office door: pay call would be held at four that afternoon. He knew that everyone had read it, but he let it stay up anyway.

Arness and another man came through the wagon gate and walked across the compound. Owen Gates was identifiable by the badge on his coat. He followed Arness one pace behind, in the manner of a man who has always had a subordinate role in life. He was middle-aged, rather thin and wan looking. Travis stepped aside so they could enter his office, and Arness introduced Gates, who shook hands halfheartedly, seeming embarrassed to be there at all. He had the uncertain manner of a man who hadn't made up his own mind in years.

"Ben told me all about the trouble," he said, sitting down. He wore a dense mustache that dripped past the ends of his mouth, and he kept brushing this with his forefinger as though it bothered him. His hat was balanced on his knees and he kept looking around the room and blowing out his breath between compressed lips. "I've been sheriff seven years now. Never had any trouble with settlers. Fact is, I never have trouble with anybody."

"Well," Travis said, "I'm just curious enough to want a look in a man's barn when he becomes overly obstinate about my not having a look in it." He regarded Owen Gates steadily. "How many men do you have in jail now?"

"Why, I don't have anybody," Gates said, surprised. "As a law officer I got other duties besides throwing people in jail. Most of the time I'm busy serving papers

36

for General Wrigley; he's got plenty of business for me to take care of."

A fringed-top buggy wheeled through the gate and came on across the yard, its brightly painted wheels sparkling. An impressive-looking man dismounted and tied the horse, then came in the office. He wore an expensive dark suit and an embroidered vest accented by a heavy gold watch chain. Thomas C. Wrigley was sixty, but still as trim as a young sapling. He had a deeply lined face and hair that was almost white. A thick mustache hid his mouth completely; he was like an historical painting, vivid in every detail, with a noble brow and a stern, unforgiving jaw.

"Mr. Travis, I believe. General Thomas C. Wrigley, C.S.A." His handshake was firm, but very brief. Then he swept his coattails aside and sat down, seeming to dominate the room with his commanding presence. "I think we'd better get right to the matter, sir. Regrettable, but not beyond salvaging." This man obviously enjoyed his role of public benefactor. His every word and gesture were calculated to show that his life was dedicated to the public cause, regardless of any inconvenience to himself.

"You're referring to the death of Oney Rink, sir?" Travis asked politely.

Wrigley frowned as though annoyed. "Of course I'm referring to Oney Rink. What a tragedy! And they were doing quite well too. Another five years and they'd have been clear of debts."

"How, sir? By selling army horses?"

"I hardly think that's the case," Wrigley said, his voice edgy. "A mistake is a mistake. It need go no farther, sir." He spread his hands briefly. "I am willing to put the whole thing aside as an impetuous error on

37

your part, sir. The last time I talked to Major Deacon he assured me that the army's position is one of protection toward the settlers. Not of enforcement. In the future, if you suspect irregularities, please report them to the sheriff and they will be duly investigated. He is employed to handle these matters."

Travis shook his head, "General, I get the distinct impression that you want this to be entirely my fault and that you're looking for a tail to tie the can to." He pointed to Owen Gates. "Has he ever arrested anyone?" He watched the color come into Gates' face, then he laughed. "Never mind, general, you don't need to answer. I'm not really interested in your sheriff. But you intrigue me, sir. I understand that you are the president of The Dixie Land Development Company. I've never met a land speculator before."

"President and owner, sir," Wrigley said. "It's my dream, my ambition, to see the vast fertile prairie populated by hardy pioneer stock, Mr. Travis. I envision schools and churches and fine homes and waving fields of grain, and I—"

"It's not necessary to make a stump speech in my office," Jefferson Travis said quietly, then he watched the amazement turn to anger in Thomas C. Wrigley's eyes. "General, I've just ridden over some of your fertile prairie, if you are referring to that dry, dusty, heat-seared section of country running all the way into north Kansas. And I find your reference to hardy pioneer stock a little amusing, if you're holding up the Rinks as an example." Travis' boyish cheeks tightened against the bones and his jaw seemed to square somewhat; he placed his hands flat against the surface of the desk and hoped that he looked like an officer capable of making a decision. "I understand my duties quite well, sir. And I also understand that there are strong factions here pulling every dangling political string in favor of the settlers, the hunters, or the Indians. I trust, general, that there is nothing in your company that cannot bear looking into."

"You'll find everything legal, sir," Wrigley said stiffly. He glanced at Ben Arness as though he thought he were being betrayed and blew out an aggravated breath. "Bless me, Mr. Travis, I came here to make friends, not split hairs. I need cooperation, sir, not irascibility. If you're going to spend your time turning up rocks to see what's under them, why—" He left the rest unsaid and stood up. "Perhaps we can talk again, after you've been here awhile. After you get a true perspective of conditions here." He tapped Owen Gates on the arm. "Come along. I've got some papers I want you to serve."

Gates went out and got in Wrigley's buggy, and they turned out of the yard. Arness sighed and scratched his head. "Did you have to make him mad, sir? He's doing a lot for this country. He's a good man, once you get to know him."

"Has he put you in his pocket too?" Travis asked. He saw a stain of red flood the sergeant's neck, then Arness gave him a blunt, angry stare.

"No," Arness said quickly. "I just do my job, sir."

Travis continued to study him, wondering if Arness was telling the truth or not. Then he said; "How did Wrigley acquire the land to form his company, sergeant?"

"Squatters' rights, mostly," Arness said. "Wrigley used to range cattle there before the war, and he had a treaty-lease agreement with the Indians. When the settlers started coming in, they had to go to Wrigley.

Some proved up on the land, but couldn't make a go of it, so he bought those out, five cents on the dollar. The rest he subleases. It's just good business, sir."

"Yes, from the cut of his clothes and the price of that rig he drives, I'd say that business was very good." He got up and put on his kepi. "Is there a doctor in town? I think I'll have this arm dressed properly."

"Yes, sir. Doc Summers lives down the street."

"I'll write my report this afternoon, sergeant. How often does the Fort Winthrop stage come through?"

"Every Friday, sir. If you're not back by pay call, sir, shall I—"

"I'll be back," Travis said, and went out.

He wondered if he had made a hasty decision regarding General Wrigley, but he had seen at once that Wrigley wanted him "on his side," and Travis realized that would never do. The minute he started to play favorites, he was finished as a commander of a functioning unit, and on the way to being through as a man. He felt a sense of pride that he had had the acumen to appraise Wrigley as a favor-seeker, a man who lived and worked along that twilight fringe of legality, taking more from the people and land than he ever put back.

There was a sign hanging near Doctor Walter Summers' gate, and as Jefferson Travis passed through and went up the walk, he suspected that a woman lived there; the carefully nurtured flowers and shrubs were evidence of this, also the crisp curtains that hung at the parlor windows. There was even a marble bird bath in the middle of the front lawn.

He knocked and heard a light step in the hall; then the door opened and a girl stood there, frankly examining him.

"I've never seen you before," she said. "Oh, you've

been hurt! Come in. The doctor will be along in a minute." She took his good arm and tenderly led him down the hall, giving him the impression that she suspected he might faint at any moment. He opened his mouth to protest this solicitude, but she didn't give him a chance. "You're very young to be an officer. I suppose you've taken charge of the detail here. Have you been in the army long?" She made him sit down and then removed the crude bandage. "My, that's ugly, isn't it? I don't suppose you put anything on it. Men never think of such things, you know. Or else they put something smelly on like the Indians use."

He studied her while she chattered, for she was a charming girl. She was somewhere between eighteen and twenty; a delightful age where being exact about it really didn't matter. Her hair was dark and shiny and her eyes were large and expressive; he imagined that she wept easily, but rarely because of herself. She moved her delicate hands with quick grace, and when he smiled at her, she smiled back.

"The doctor will have to take some stitches in that, lieutenant. If the pain bothers you, I can let you have a drink of whiskey." He shook his head and she frowned. "Wouldn't you like a drink? Men usually do, you know. Doctor Summers says it's the first rule of medicine; give them a good drink and let nature take its course."

An elderly man stepped into the room, shrugging into his coat. He had a pipe locked between his teeth, and he puffed on it. After a glance at Travis' uniform and rank, he said, "Mmmm. Kind of messy, isn't it? Give you much trouble?" He prodded the flesh around the wound with his finger and Jefferson Travis gripped the arm of the chair tightly to keep from flinching. "Pretty tender. We'll wash it out with peroxide and close it."

"I'm Lieutenant Jefferson Travis, doctor."

Summers looked at him for a moment, as though wondering what the point was. "You get this from the Rinks?" He nodded toward the wound.

"News travels fast," Travis said. "Well, he shot me first."

Summers turned to the cabinet for a bottle, a swab, and a surgical sewing kit. "Fetch me a pan of water, Hope." He soaked the swab with peroxide and washed the wound carefully. "The Rinks are wild all right. They ran Ben Arness off once." He placed Travis' arm straight out. "This might hurt a little."

When the needle bit in, Travis realized what an understatement the doctor had made. He bit his lip and stiffened, and sweat popped out on his forehead, but he managed to keep his mouth shut. Hope wiped his face twice, then Summers was finished.

"Hope will bandage that," he said. "Shall I send the army the bill? It's only two dollars."

"I'll pay it," Travis said.

"Come back in a week and let me have a look at it," Summers said, and went out.

Hope wrapped his arm and he sat there and observed the play of sunlight on her cheeks and bare arms. "Is your name Hope Summers?"

"Hope Randall. Doctor Summers is my mother's brother." She finished with his arm and was going to make a sling for it, but he shook his head.

"I'm not going to baby this," he said, rolling down his sleeve. "Would you tell me something if I asked you?"

"You'd have to ask me first."

"I got the impression from Doctor Summers that I'm more to blame than the Rinks for what happened."

Her expression became serious for a moment. "Mr.

42

Travis, it's hard for us to really blame those people for anything. They have nothing at all, and so little prospect of getting anything. So when they steal a horse or a buffalo hide, or a steer, we secretly hope they'll get away with it. Not that it's right to steal. But it's less than right to have so little, and we're always sorry, just a little bit, when they get caught. If being blamed bothers you, Mr. Travis, then you ought to get another assignment. You're always going to be blamed; that's what you're here for. There are cattlemen here who'll blame you for not killing all the Rinks, and General Wrigley's settlers will blame you for being in the pay of the cattlemen, or the Indian agent, or the buffalo hunters, who sometimes come this far south. Do you understand how it is? You can't be fair. Ben Arness tried it, but he had to decide who he was for. Sooner or later, you'll have to swing over to one side or the other."

"And what if I don't?"

"You won't be able to help yourself," she said. Then she smiled. "Come back next Wednesday."

After pay call, Ben Arness walked to the edge of town and cut across a vacant lot, walking toward a scatter of adobes. The largest of these was four rooms with a porch running around all sides, and he went around to the rear patio. Strong poles had been set into the ground and ropes tightly strung, and from these hung enough washing to supply a regiment. A woman worked over a scrubboard, sweat coursing down her face and soaking the shoulders of her dress. A small girl helped her, folding clothes in a large basket while a boy of eleven stoked the fire, keeping the kettles of water hot. This was her living, at ten cents a bundle, and the work went on six days a week.

The girl saw Arness first and ran toward him; he

43

scooped her up in his arms and carried her back. Grace Beaumont snapped her hands to fling off the soapsuds, then wiped them on her apron. She was a small woman, touching thirty, dark-haired and dark-eyed. Her face was round and ruddy from near constant exposure to the sun, and her hands were always chapped from immersion in hot water and strong soap.

To the boy, Arness said, "Let the fire go for a while, son."

"What you got in the saddlebag?" the boy asked.

"Something," Arness said, and sat down on the porch step where there was a little shade. The girl climbed on his knee and Grace Beaumont shooed her off.

"Ben doesn't want you pestering him."

"It's all right," Arness said, and picked up his saddlebag. He produced a doll first and gave it to the girl, and she hugged him and kissed his cheek. Linsay Beaumont was disgusted at this feminine display and snorted through his nose. The girl went into the house with her doll, humming to it.

"That's the first pretty thing she's had in a long spell, Ben. And it was mighty thoughtful of you."

"Here's a jackknife for you," Arness said, handing it to the boy.

"Gosh!" He dashed off for a piece of wood.

Arness hesitated. "I bought you something and I want you to take it without any fuss now." He showed her a bolt of blue velveteen and she put both hands to her mouth and gasped. Then she shook her head.

"I can't take it, Ben. Lord knows, I want to, but I can't."

"Why?"

She smiled wistfully. "If I made a dress of it, people would see it and know I didn't buy it here. They'd guess

44

where I got it. But it was a lovely thought, Ben. One I'll remember."

He took off his hat and sighed. "I see you scrub your knuckles raw to earn seven dollars a week, and you tell me you can't have something pretty? You keep it. Maybe you can't use it, but you keep it and look at it and feel it once in awhile, just to remind you there's other things in the world besides sweat and disappointment."

"All right, Ben." She caressed the cloth and smiled. "Someday I might make a dress of it." She studied him carefully, detecting a worry in his expression that hadn't been there before. "Ben, what's the matter? You look discouraged. Is there something wrong?"

He spoke softly. "That new lieutenant asked me a question a few hours ago. He asked me if General Wrigley had me in his pocket, and I said no. But I didn't want to lie to him, Grace." He slapped his leg angrily. "Twenty-seven years a soldier, and a kid makes me ashamed of myself."

"Ben, don't be so hard, so unbending. Isn't it time you gave it up?"

He looked at her. "Get out? No. No, I couldn't do that. I don't want to talk about it, Grace." He shook his head. "I'll see it through, because I've been in too long to throw it all away. Travis won't get a chance to bust me in rank. No fresh-faced kid's going to steal twenty-seven years from me, Grace."

"What makes you think he will, Ben?" Her voice was quiet.

He looked at her, suddenly embarrassed. "No reason," he mumbled, and added quickly, "Well, I'd better get back before I give him one. I'll see you soon." He turned and walked rapidly back to the barracks.

45

4

In making out his report, Jefferson Travis took the greatest care to be exact, relating every pertinent detail of the affair at the Rinks' soddy. He offered no excuses or apologies and made no special point about recovering the two horses, although he included a description of them, identifying them positively by the company and regiment number cut into the hooves.

Placing the report in a small dispatch pouch, he sent a trooper to the express office with it to see that it got into the Fort Winthrop mail pouch. He was bone-tired, so he slept for a while, had a late supper, then went out and sat on the porch, hoping that a night breeze would come up to cut the heat rising from the sun-soaked ground.

Sergeant Arness came into the compound; he did not see Travis sitting there to one side of the porch. But when Travis spoke, Arness came over and stood in the shaft of dull lamplight streaming out of the doorway.

"Sit down, sergeant," Travis said. "We'd better have a talk."

"What about, sir?"

"About your twenty-seven year contract with the army. It seems that your long service has given you the idea that you can run things to suit yourself. I'm not going to assume that you *knew* there were horses concealed in the Rinks' barn, sergeant, or that you were *willing* to pass up an opportunity to recover them. But at the same time, I'm going to have to take with a grain of salt all I've been told about you being such a good soldier. 'The best damned sergeant in the army,' as it was put to me. So far you've proved to be no more than a recalcitrant crank with a peckish grudge against

46

anyone who doesn't believe the army is a great career. I don't feel that I have to put up with it. Do you understand?"

"Yes, sir. May I speak freely, lieutenant?"

"Go ahead. I'm not going to pull my rank on you."

Arness took off his hat and folded the brim back so that it was a roll of felt in his hands. "I've been running this detail without an officer and with no complaints from the major, sir. And no Academy-green officer can do any better. I'm not going to claim that I don't favor the homesteaders, because I do. But I do know what's good for this country and you don't. You keep on the way you're going and all the work I've done will be wasted. The buffalo hunters are guttin' the country, sir. And the Indians, they don't bring anything but misery; the sooner they're gone or held on reservation, the better off everyone will be. Wrigley's trying to open up the country, promote a railroad, and get people to settle the land. I made up my mind some time ago as to who was doing the most good. You want to bust me, court-martial me for that, then you go right ahead."

"Hell, man, we're not talking about disciplinary action," Travis said. "If you'd stop for five minutes and forget that you're a twenty-seven year man, you might remember the job you're here to do." He fell silent for a moment, then said, "From the way Gates and Wrigley talked, I knew that you favored their action. Of course, nothing openly; you think too much of your stripes to run any risks. Now, you may consider that clever as hell, but I consider it much less. As far as I'm concerned you've never had nerve enough to take a stand for fear you'd lose your precious chevrons." He turned his head and looked at Ben Arness. "But the fence-straddling is over, sergeant. You realize that, don't you? I'm going to

47

give it to you straight: you soldier with me, my way, or I'll send you back to Fort Winthrop. Make up your mind."

"What do you know about soldiering, sir? Hell, the creases ain't out of your uniform yet." He slapped his hat on his head. "All you know about the army is what you learned at the Academy out of a book. Well I learned mine firsthand, sir. The only way to learn. And there's a hell of a difference in what I already know and what you've got to learn."

"You're right," Travis said. "And I'll point out one of those differences right now, sergeant. You like to think of yourself as a first-class sergeant, a man who's always had his duty and done it. The truth is that you're as much a slacker as the worst recruit. You haven't done army duty for a long time, sergeant. You do duty for yourself, because you can't think of anything but your long record of faithful service. What do you want, a testimonial from the area commander? It's a big army and it was working fine long before you came along, and it'll do just as well after you're gone. Your army, sergeant?" He smiled and shook his head. "Ten days after your retirement retreat the army won't even remember your name." He got up and brushed off the seat of his pants. "I want the detail mounted and ready to leave at seven, sergeant. Rations for five days and regular ammunition issue."

He stood there while Arness walked away, and he wondered how wise it had been to lay it on the line that way. Whether he liked Arness or not, he needed him; an officer was nothing without his sergeant, next to helpless. Yet it made Travis angry when an enlisted man used that as a wedge to get his own way. Somehow, and he didn't know how, he would have to win Arness over.

48

Or get rid of him entirely. But that would look bad, for himself and Arness; just because they didn't get along was no reason to blot his record.

The whole thing irritated and upset him; he hated a bad start, and this was not good. Well, it would take time and some thinking out. He had no intention of making a hasty decision.

He thought about going to bed, but it was too early, and he wouldn't be able to sleep anyway. Activity was what he needed, something to take his mind off his problems, and he thought about going to the Summers house. He could test the cordiality of his welcome, and if it was cool, he could say that his bandage was too tight and that he'd like it changed.

And if it wasn't cool? He found that possibility rather pleasant. He felt the need of something pleasant to take his mind off Arness.

As he walked along the dark street he told himself that he was being foolish going to the doctor's house on the off chance that he would see Hope Randall. But he'd always been pretty foolish where attractive girls were concerned, and he saw no reason to change now.

A lamp was lit in the parlor, though the rest of the house was dark. He thought of turning around and going back, but it wasn't in his nature to turn back from the things he started. As he stepped on the porch he realized that someone was sitting there.

"Doctor Summers?"

"He's at a cattlemen's meeting at the hotel," Hope said. "You can wait for him, if you like. I was just going to have some lemonade. You'd like some, wouldn't you?"

He was going to say that he would, but she got up and went into the house, returning a moment later with a

49

pitcher and glasses. "It certainly was hot today, wasn't it? A hundred and three by the thermometer." She handed him a glass and he perched on the porch railing so he faced her. The light was faint here, just enough to break the solidness of night.

"The cattlemen called the meeting as soon as they heard you recovered those two horses from the Rinks."

"I don't get the connection," Travis said.

"Why, it's simple. You got the horses back, and it's been a long time since anything was recovered from the homesteaders. They steal all the time from the cattlemen, but with Owen Gates working for Wrigley, and Ben sympathizing—I suppose I shouldn't have said that." Then she shrugged. "But you're bright enough to have figured it out anyway. You can't blame Ben, Mr. Travis; he wants to marry Grace Beaumont."

"That's a reason?"

She laughed. "That did sound a little disjointed, didn't it? She and her husband tried dry farming. Hard work killed him, then she came to town. It's natural for Ben to feel as he does, being in love with her. You certainly don't talk much, do you?"

"Not when it means interrupting," he said.

"All right," she said, laughing. "So I chatter. My mother chattered, and Aunt Clara did too. She lived with us, but she never married. And it was a shame too. She was a wonderful cook. But father said she would have talked a man into his grave. What's your first name?"

"Jeff," he said. "And you're never going to be an old maid, Hope."

She laughed musically. "Well, I'm glad to hear that. I guess it wouldn't matter anyway, but people make such a thing of it, as if it was some secret sin, and they spend

50

all their time trying to figure out what's wrong with you that you couldn't get a man. What made you go into the army? Were you unhappy at home?"

He shook his head helplessly. "You make good lemonade, Hope. Where did you get the ice to cool it?"

"Oh, there isn't any ice," she said. "You wrap the pitcher in a cloth, set it in a pan, then saturate the cloth with ether. It evaporates so rapidly that it makes the pitcher cold."

"A scientist," he said, jokingly. "My respect increases by the moment." He raised his glass in salute. "To cool lemonade on the front porch. I grew up on a front porch, you know. It was just a straight line to the cookie jar, which mother always hid in the hall closet. Cookies were precious in my family. She never knew that I knew where it was."

"I'll make some cookies if you like."

He quickly put out his hand, as though expecting her to leap up and make them that very moment. She laughed and said, "I meant the day after tomorrow."

"Could you make it next week? I'm going to take a patrol to the reservation." He took out his watch and looked at it. "I've overstayed my welcome. Thank you for the talk. I'll be back for the cookies."

"Cinnamon or sugar?"

"Do you know how to make gingersnaps?"

"Yes." She offered her hand and he took it and bowed gallantly and touched his lips to it in a most courtly, continental manner.

He whistled softly as he walked back to the barracks, and when he took off his boots, getting ready for bed, he stopped and stared at the wall for a moment, then laughed and shook his head. He was still smiling when he turned out the lamp and squirmed to find a comfortable sleeping position.

Before ten o'clock Lieutenant Jefferson Travis, trailed by Sergeant Arness and fourteen troopers, splashed across the river north of Spanish Spring, and approached Regan's trading post, a low, log building nestled in a cottonwood grove. Regan heard their approach and came out as they dismounted in his yard. A trooper took charge of the horses while the detail rested.

Regan was a man of indeterminable age. His place was a catchall for trading with the Indians, and his store and yard as untidy as he was. Regan shaved when he thought about it, which wasn't often, and he made it a practice to wear his shirt and pants until they became too dirty even for him to bear, then he threw them away, about once a year, and put on new ones. It probably never occurred to him to bathe first. There was a wild varmint odor about him and the trading post, and Travis wrinkled his nose in distaste as he stepped inside.

"I guess you be the new officer," Regan said, smiling, offering his hand. "Howdy, Ben. Ain't seen you for a month. Whiskey inside, if you want it."

Travis glanced at Arness and found the man's face quite red. "No, Mr. Regan, the sergeant isn't accepting gratuities today. Let me see your government permit to operate this boar's nest."

This insulted Regan. "I ain't had any complaints. Ask the Indian agent."

"I will," Travis said. "Let's see the papers."

Regan could not immediately find his trading permit. He searched through old cigar boxes under the counter, then finally came up with it. Travis looked at it and found that the yearly endorsements were there, and that it had been signed by the commander at Fort Dodge.

"That satisfy you?" Regan asked. He was a wizened man, like an ancient piece of leather, toughened rather than weakened by age. His hair was long and he wore a pistol in a hip holster.

"Don't you ever clean this place up?" Travis asked.

"What for? The Injuns don't mind a little dirt." He squinted at Jefferson Travis. "For a kid, you're pecky as hell, ain't you? What you want to do, get promoted the first year?" He scrubbed a hand across his dirty face. "Goddamn, ain't it bad enough for a man to try to make an honest livin' without the army pokin' around? I got a gov'mint license, sonny. I'm as important as you."

"Do you keep records?" Travis asked.

"Sure I keep records. An officer from Fort Dodge comes here every three months and checks 'em. What about it?"

"I'll take a look at them," Travis said and watched the contrariness come into Regan's face. "If you'd like, Mr. Regan, I can find them myself."

"Oh, hell, I'll get 'em," Regan said. He planked some books on the counter and looked sourly at Jefferson Travis. "But sonny, I'm sure going to write Fort Dodge about this; they'll have your ass for foolin' with me."

"Yes, you do that," Travis said. "Sergeant, would you see that a noon camp is established in the grove. Then come back in here."

"Yes, sir." He detected frost in Travis' voice and knew that he was responsible for its being there. Travis wasn't saying anything now, but Arness knew it would come later.

The complete account of Regan's trading was there, only Travis had another word for it: cheating. Two knives, some beads and a yard of cloth for one buffalo

53

robe; he thought this was the most outrageous swindle he had ever heard of, yet that seemed to be the going rate. Regan's trading was not confined to Indians; he also bought horses from time to time, and cattle, and the name of every settler within a thirty-mile radius was listed there, and the price paid for the merchandise.

Travis was a little surprised at the clear picture the records painted. He was struck right away with the oddness of all the horses being described as fifteen hands high, solid-colored, gelding; this must be army stock, bought by Regan and sold through some Dodge City contact. And surely the officer who checked these books saw this, or was totally blind.

When Arness came back inside, Travis looked pointedly at Regan until the man moved away. Then he spoke quietly, "Sergeant, have you lost any horses this past year?"

"Yes, sir. Three." He looked steadily at Travis. "I made a report of it, and a search."

"With your eyes closed?" Travis pointed to the entries. "How much would you bet that those aren't army mounts, sergeant?" He snapped the ledger closed. "Haven't you seen anything, sergeant?"

"Now don't start blaming me, sir," Arness said. "Sure, I knew Regan bought a few horses, but that never gave me the right to dispute the officers from Fort Dodge." He wiped his mouth with his hand and shifted his feet. "And if you've got any sense, you're not going to make a big fuss over this either. Major Griswald signed those ledgers, and there's one hell of a lot of difference in authority between a second lieutenant and a major." He reached out and tapped Lieutenant Travis on the chest. "Dodge is headquarters for the buffalo hunters. And the officers at Fort Dodge know what side

54

their bread's buttered on. Ah, sir, you're going to get yourself busted right out of the army before you get started. What do you expect, sir, everybody to live by the Golden Rule? There ain't a man in a hundred miles who don't have an ax to grind. You'd better start sharpening your own, sir."

"Which faction would you suggest I join, sergeant? You seem to favor several."

"I've never seen a man so pigheaded," Arness snapped. "All right, do as you damned please. You will anyway."

"Thank you for seeing it," Travis said softly. "Get the detail mounted, sergeant. We're going on to the reservation headquarters."

Arness smiled with relief. "That's more like it, sir. Hell, what good would it do to make a fuss about Regan; they'd just put somebody else here as crooked as he is."

"That's true," Travis said. "That's why I'm going to padlock the place and confiscate the records. Will you see that Corporal Busik attends to it?"

Arness was too furious to answer; he stomped out and a moment later Regan came in, anger staining his dark cheeks.

"You can't close me!"

"I'll give you five minutes to gather your personal belongings," Travis told him. "You can make your complaints at Fort Dodge."

"And you can damned sure bet I will!" Regan shouted, and began to throw a bedroll together.

Travis went outside just as a trooper called from the river crossing, and he looked that way; four mounted men were splashing across. They came directly toward Regan's yard and this gave him a moment to study them. They were sun-browned men, and all of them wore suits and wide hats, spike-heeled boots with Mexican rowel spurs and pistols on their hips; the cattleman stamp was on them.

They drew up in a swirl of dust and dismounted. One of them said, "I'm Janeway, Circle T. This is Hodges, Rider, and Butram. We heard you pulled out early this morning and hoped we'd catch you."

"Well, you have, gentlemen," Travis said. Corporal Busik went around Regan's place, locking the doors while two other troopers nailed boards over the windows.

"You closing him?" Janeway asked. Then he laughed and slapped his side and turned to the others. "By God, it's about time, ain't it?" He looked again at Travis. "Well, I always said we'd get something done if an officer took over. Every damned year there's a hundred head of beef crossing that river with homesteaders right behind them. I'll bet we wrote a dozen letters to the army asking them to do something about those thieves, and it looks like we're finally getting results."

"I wasn't aware that you had written letters," Travis said. "And as far as closing Mr. Regan, I did so for military reasons."

Janeway looked disappointed and puzzled. "Well, now, wait a minute. From the way you handled the Rinks, we thought—" He looked at his friends. "I guess we were wrong."

"I haven't chosen a side," Travis said. "And gentlemen, I don't intend to. Why don't you try to get along with the settlers?"

"What?" Janeway reared back. "Sonny, every waterhole they squat around is a waterhole we can no longer use. By God, if it gets much worse—we're going to get up a Winchester and hemp party!"

"If you do that, Mr. Janeway, the army will come after you and hang you."

"Let's get out of here," Hodges said. "We're wasting our time." They stepped into their saddles, and Hodges said, "I can see how it is, sonny. It figures that you'd be more ambitious than Ben. We could never count on him because of the Beaumont woman. Not that way with you though, is it? You'll side with the money, the buffalo hunters and the bunch at Fort Dodge."

"Good day, gentlemen," Travis said with careful civility.

Janeway snapped, "Well, you don't deny it. I give you credit for that." He wheeled his horse then and headed for the crossing, the others right behind him.

Regan was saddling a horse when Travis mounted his detail and swung to the northwest toward the Indian reservation headquarters. On the hour they paused to dismount and walk the horses, and every two hours there was a fifteen minute halt for housekeeping. It was during this time that Jefferson Travis sat down beside Arness.

"I was too generous with you last night at the barracks, sergeant. I offered you a chance to get along. If I had any sense I'd send a dispatch to Fort Winthrop and have you recalled." He studied Arness. "And if you want to know the truth of it, sergeant, I wouldn't miss you a damned bit. It would be a relief to let some other officer wear you around his neck."

"I figured you'd duck behind that little gold bar when it got tough," Arness said softly, so that no one else heard.

"What did you do," Travis asked, "make a bet on it?" He got up and took off his neckerchief, throwing it on

57

the ground. "No one has ever really taught you respect, sergeant. I'm not talking about respect for a man, but for rank. You've never admitted that Congress makes the officers, not Ben Arness." He slipped out of his shirt and dropped it to the ground, and a trooper saw him and nudged another, and this went on until they were all watching. Unbuckling his belt, Travis lowered pistol, saber, and bullet pouch to the ground. "Do you know what's eating you? You secretly detest all officers and wish the army could get along without them. Or perhaps you want to play the old army game of hiding behind your stripes. Enlisted men do that, sergeant. When they're alone with an officer, they get insulting with their mouths, and other times they just fool around on the fringe of insubordination, or get balky in the ranks. You know I could get court-martialed for offering to fight an enlisted man, but that would be better than listening to any more of your jibes." He pointed to his shirt. "The rank's there, sergeant. What are you going to do about it?"

One of the men said, "Why don't you take him, Ben? He's beggin' for it."

Travis wasn't sure whether this swung Arness or whether he'd decided before the man spoke; anyway he began to peel off his shirt and sidearms. "Did you take boxing lessons at the Academy, sir? You'll need 'em."

"A little," Travis said. "But I was captain of the wrestling team for two years."

"That's nice," Arness said, and swung, and in the blow was all his resentment and pent-up hostility. Travis twisted and the fist bounced off his shoulder, then he chopped a blow to Arness' mouth and sent him staggering back, feet pawing the grass for purchase. Travis hadn't hit him hard, but he'd hit fast; the fist had

58

just flicked out and found the target.

The first blood brought caution to Arness, then he whirled in, arms windmilling. Travis stood like a rooted tree until the last moment, then he whipped aside, blocked Arness' rush with an out-thrust foot and sent him sprawling.

He got up quickly and eyed Travis, then he came in low and bull-rushed the slender young man. He hooked Travis under the heart and in the face, knocking him to one side so that Travis had to stagger to catch his balance. He kicked and missed, then Travis got in close, his arms embracing Ben Arness. There was a flick of his hip and Arness sailed to the dust and rolled away.

Suddenly Travis altered his tactics and went for Arness as soon as he came erect. He caught an arm, twisted it, put his shoulder in place, and flipped Arness into the air. A bomb of dust arose when Arness struck, and he grunted as the breath was all but knocked from him. This time Travis fell on him and there was a moment of snake thrashing.

This stopped suddenly and Arness gave an agonized cry. Travis had one hand in his hair, cruelly pulling his head back. One of Arness' arms was brutally twisted behind his back, securely locked; he was held in a posture of pain, and quite calmly Jefferson Travis said, "We settle it now, sergeant. Twenty-seven years of mule stubbornness is going to go. Either I command or you do, and I know which it's going to be, but I want you to say it. I want you to know it and live with it."

He applied pressure and Arness groaned loudly, then between ragged breaths he said, "You do—sir."

He released Arness and turned to his clothes and started to put them on. The troopers were silent, and he fully understood why. They did not applaud his victory;

rather they resented it, for he had taken a man they had admired and trusted and humbled him. And Arness could only genuinely hate him for it. The only one he had proved anything to was himself, and he wondered now if it had really been necessary. He really didn't need Ben Arness' scalp to be a man.

5

TRAVIS' DESTINATION WAS THE INDIAN RESERVATION, and he made a slow night march toward it. He rode at the head of the column, jumping jack rabbits from the brush and startling small game. A wind came up which helped to blow the dust they raised away from them, and after three hours of this he ordered a two-hour rest.

Lieutenant Jefferson Travis then spent a great deal of time in soul-searching introspection. He knew that only time would correct his youth, but he could not always reconcile himself to patience. Since beginning his military career, he had tried only to obey the dictates of his conscience and the inflexible commandments of Army regulations, and in this respect he felt that he had done tolerably well. But his relationship with Sergeant Arness was badly awry, and he had succeeded in aggravating two of the factions wrestling for dominance in his district. None of this would set well with Major Deacon, but thinking about it, Travis decided he could not afford to feel concerned over this. To choose a side, a man had to feel that all the right was on one side and all the wrong on the other, but he couldn't see any such clear-cut division in this instance. He could not really blame the settlers for stealing since he knew how desperately poor they were, but still he recognized his responsibility to curtail this thievery.

As far as the sergeant and Major Deacon were concerned, he did not feel compelled to conform to their formula of a typical career officer, and perhaps, Travis reasoned, this was his biggest mistake. Perhaps he should try to attain this peculiar mental attitude, this state of aloof detachment which seemed to be necessary to get him through his first tour of duty with the least amount of unpleasantness, and if by such neglect he left behind certain loose ends, the next officer, who might be more seasoned, would take care of them.

The detail made an early morning approach to the agency headquarters, passing east of the sprawling Indian village. Nestled in a hollow, with trees and a spring, headquarters was a long adobe with a scattering of outbuildings. A flagpole marked the agent's office, and as Travis brought his detail closer he saw an army escort wagon and some cavalry mounts tied by the stable. A half-dozen soldiers lounged in the shade of the blacksmith shop, watching as Travis dismounted his troop and turned it over to Ben Arness.

Mr. Brewer, the agent, came out as Travis stepped to the porch. He was a short, scholarly man in his middle thirties, and in spite of the heat he wore a dark suit with a vest under the coat. His handshake was perfunctory; he presented only a surface politeness and from this Travis deducted that Mr. Brewer had no love for the army, which was natural since he represented the Interior Department. Now he said, apparently amiably, "Come inside. It's cooler there." From the man's manner, Travis suspected that he wasn't particularly well suited to this job, but that he tried to do what was expected of him, probably writing letters to Washington begging for more help, more money, and less army interference. And Travis saw with detached clarity what Mr. Brewer did not see at all: that he was a man destined to lose. The taxpayers would always accuse him of graft, the army would accuse him of ignorance, and his own superiors, bowing to the policy of the moment, would accuse him of incompetence.

Meanwhile, the Indians would take his handouts as long as they lasted, and in the end desert him, for they wasted no loyalty on white men.

Travis looked around the pleasant room, thinking that Brewer had it nice. There were Mexican rugs on the floor, drapes at the windows, and substantial furniture, better than most colonels found in Quarters "A." There were many Indian artifacts. Evidently Brewer was a collector, taking pleasure in the primitive craft of the people around him.

"Major Griswald is here from Fort Dodge," Brewer said. "He's in my office. Would you care for some wine?" He opened a door and ushered Travis in ahead of him. Griswald was sorting through some papers; he looked around, saw Travis, then put the papers aside and stood up. He was a large man, with a rather flat face and a dense mustache, clipped short. His eyes were wide spaced and bland.

"Travis, from Spanish Spring?" Griswald asked. "This meeting is unexpected. I hope there's no trouble. Goes in the report, you know."

"Just getting familiar with the territory, sir." He offered his hand. "Glad to meet you, sir."

Mr. Brewer was closing his liquor cabinet; he had three glasses of wine on a small silver tray. "Won't you sit down, Mr. Travis." He folded his hands together and looked from one to the other. "Well," he said, "I don't usually have so much company."

"Mr. Travis," Griswald said, "I don't want you to think I'm infringing on your territory by being here. As it happened, Mr. Brewer and I met briefly last year in St. Louis, and every time I go south to Regan's crossing, I always stop and visit." He laughed softly. "You're obviously new to the army, Mr. Travis, but one thing we never do is to mind another officer's duty. I take it you crossed at Regan's."

"Yes, sir," Travis said. "However, I might save you the trouble of the ride. I imagine he's now headed for Fort Dodge, sir. You see, I closed his place because he was buying stolen army horses."

Major Andrew Griswald had been sipping his wine; he stopped but still held the glass to his lips. He looked at Jefferson Travis as though he had not really seen him before, then he put the glass aside. "Did I understand you correctly, Mr. Travis?"

"I'm sure you did, sir. The army has been losing horses from time to time, and everyone seems to be aware that the settlers are taking them to sell rather than returning them to the army. I recovered two horses myself before they could be sold, and I found entries in Regan's books showing that he'd bought six this past year. And so it will go in my report."

"By God," Griswald snapped, "you have a cool manner, I must say. I'm going to write to your commanding officer about this, Mr. Travis. As far as the army is concerned, Jack Regan is an honest man, and I consider your action in this matter quite impertinent." He slapped his hands together in exasperation. "Dammit, I've personally inspected his accounts and in my opinion they are quite legitimate. And I'm not going to alter my opinion, regardless of what you may think." He calmed himself by drinking the rest of his wine. "Mr. Travis, you're new to the army. Perhaps you didn't realize when you closed Regan that you would place the military in an embarrassing position."

"On the contrary, I gave it every consideration, major. In fact, sir, Regan threatened me at some length, claiming friends in high places." He glanced at Brewer.

"This is good wine."

"Just one of the social graces I've tried to preserve," Brewer said wistfully. "It's difficult to remain civilized out here. And it's not often I entertain men who appreciate the good things." His anxious expression showed that he hoped his guests would find a more amiable topic.

"Hang your social fetishes, Brewer!" Griswald snapped ungraciously. He got up and walked around the room, then went to the window and stood there, looking into the yard, and beyond, to the Indian camp. "Mr. Travis, you seem to be a sensible young man. I don't want to have to write a report in rebuttal that will affect your future. Do you follow me?"

"Yes, sir," Travis said.

Griswald turned and looked with some irritation at Brewer. "Aren't you having a beef issue tomorrow? We don't want to detain you from your duties."

"Well, I have nothing—" Brewer stopped, then nodded. He was a gentle man, preferring to absorb rudeness rather than create more unpleasantness. "Of course, major. You'll stay for supper this evening, won't you, Mr. Travis?"

He went out and closed the door, and Griswald said, "Stupid ass! He'd be more at home serving tea in a parlor instead of beef to the Indians. God knows why the Department sends men like that out here." Then he turned to his chair and sat down. "Army business, Mr. Travis, is best talked over among army men." He brought out a cigar case and offered one. "Have you been fighting, Mr. Travis? There are several bruises on your face. Well, it's no matter. Not in my jurisdiction." He shook his finger at Travis. "That's a very important point, sir: jurisdiction. In spite of its proximity to

Spanish Spring, Regan's trading post is in my jurisdiction, while the agency here is in yours. I suppose I could make sense of it, but I'm not being paid to. Ah, well, you'll hear your share of complaints, Mr. Travis. And be sure to note them very carefully, then forget them. There isn't a time that I come here when Brewer doesn't get on me about the buffalo hunters taking over the Indians' grassland and hunting ground. How can you argue with him? It's true, the Indians were pushed back, and some say it's unjust, but say what you will, we brought roads and towns. It's progress, Mr. Travis. Buffalo hides built Dodge City and they're paying for the railroad now." He tapped ash from his cigar. "What do the Indians pay for? Nothing! They cost money. And the sod-busters?" He chuckled. "Mr. Travis, if you went around and gathered up all the money they have, it wouldn't stake you to a good Dodge City poker game. Are you beginning to understand what I'm talking about, Mr. Travis?"

"Yes, sir," Travis said. "It's quite clear. The homesteaders have to go because they're poor, and the Indians because they're in the way. It's a very defined policy, sir. Hardly fair, but well defined."

Major Andrew Griswald frowned. "You have a damned blunt tongue, Mr. Travis. I'm sure the general wouldn't put it quite like that, even in the company of his closest associates. You apparently haven't learned how to get along in the army, and I advise you to correct that immediately." He shifted in his chair and crossed his legs. "I assume we can consider the matter of Jack Regan closed? I'll send him back and you can strike the lock off the door."

"Very well, sir," Travis said stiffly. "But if he buys another stolen horse, or a rustled steer, I'll have him

66

thrown in jail."

Brewer came back into the room before the major could explode. Griswald clamped his cigar between his teeth and said, "I'll see you at supper, Travis." His boots thudded on the porch, then he crossed the yard to the spring.

"He's upset very easily," Brewer said, regretfully. "I'm afraid you've disturbed him, Mr. Travis." Then, evidently seeking a more pleasant topic, he said politely, "Will you stay for the beef issue tomorrow? It's quite a barbaric spectacle; the Indians like to turn it into a hunt."

"Where do you buy your beef?"

Brewer shrugged. "Where I can get it. The cattlemen around Spanish Spring mostly, when the price is reasonable. Some of the settlers bring in a few head now and then. Never more than four or five. I'm buying from them tomorrow."

"Stolen stock, Mr. Brewer?"

"I'm not very well informed on brands, Mr. Travis."

"I see. Well, I can hardly expect that you've required a bill of sale."

"You have quarters next to mine," Brewer said evasively. "I really would like to talk to you. It's damned lonely out here, with only a trunk full of books, and the memory of a pleasant life I'll likely never resume."

"Perhaps you should have a wife," Travis suggested.

"No decent woman could bear this life," he said. He pointed to a wall map with isolated pins thrust into it. "Those are settlers' places. I've been to a few. Do you know that some of them live in caves, Mr. Travis? I've never seen such poverty. I couldn't live that way. No, there are certain amenities a man must observe, or stop being a man."

Privately Travis doubted that Brewer would ever know the meaning of the word. He wondered what weird circumstances had brought this fussy wretch out to Kansas as Indian agent. Yet, Brewer was not really corrupt or venal. Within his own pathetic limitations he evidently tried to do the best job he could. Travis was conscious of feeling both pity and impatience. Embarrassed, he rose and put on his kepi.

"Well, I'd better be off, Mr. Brewer. Many thanks for the hospitality."

The agent ducked his head. "Supper's at eight. The sun's down then and the flies aren't so thick." He paused, then added, "And we always had supper at eight at home. A man mustn't forget those things, you know."

Lieutenant Travis made a polite sound of agreement and departed to conduct an impromptu inspection of his men and mounts. He found everything in order. Arness was not going to be caught that way. The sergeant spoke to him, but only when asked a question, and he limped a little, suffering from the after-effects of the fight.

That evening, at supper, Travis tried to hold up his end of the conversation; Major Griswald was inclined to silence and excused himself early, saying that he wanted to start back to Dodge right away. His tone implied that this would have considerable significance for Jefferson Travis' future, but the young officer refused to show concern.

Brewer kept him up until nearly midnight, recounting his boyhood experiences in Pennsylvania, and his present ambitions. He wanted a career in politics, but listening to him, Travis knew that he was both too sincere and too ineffectual. Brewer's ambitions had the texture of impossible dreams. Finally, when the wine

68

bottle was empty and the lamp nearly out of coal oil, Brewer was ready to retire. Travis was already half asleep.

Before dawn, Jefferson Travis woke to the husk of the wind and got up without lighting the lamp. The minute he stepped outside he smelled the rain and knew it wouldn't be long in coming. He supposed this was the kind of weather a man had to get used to in this country, dry as a week-old cake one day and a regular gully-buster the next. He turned back inside to finish dressing and by the time he was finished the first blast hit the building.

The rain would turn the prairie into a morass, especially in the agency yard, where the dust was four inches thick. Today's beef issue would be a filthy business.

Travis ate breakfast with Brewer, then went out on the porch to watch the beef issue begin. In all, he estimated that there were five hundred Indians clustered about, away from the yard, most of them mounted and waiting with spears or bow and arrow. The women and children made a noisy knot apart from the men; they milled about calling to the children, and the dog pack, an integral part of Indian life, ran yipping among the gathered cattle, trying to spook them.

The agency employees had set up chair and tables and kept long lists of names handy. When a name was called out, a steer was released from the small herd, driven into a run, then chased and killed as buffalo were killed. The rain made a mess of the yard, and after the twentieth steer had been slaughtered the stench of blood and manure became almost unbearable. After each Indian made his kill, the women rushed out and began butchering on the spot, and soon the yard was dotted with kneeling women, covered with blood and mud, and the newly freed cattle were suffering for a place to run.

Now and then an Indian would dash through carelessly, bowling some woman over, and her man would get all steamed up about it, and then a fight would start.

Travis was paying more attention to the "cowboys" than the slaughter. Finally he stepped off the porch, splashed to the stable and got his horse. Mounted, his poncho spread about him, he rode over to where the herd was being held. As he approached, he noticed that the men moved away slightly as though he had some communicable disease and they were afraid of catching it. There was none of the "cattleman" look about them; they would have appeared more natural with hoes in their hands.

"I'm Lieutenant Travis, commanding the Spanish Spring detail," he said, facing two men. "Are these your cattle?"

"They be," one of them said. His open buckskin shirt revealed dirty underwear. Long hair fell to his shoulders in an unwashed, uncombed tangle, and one cheek was fat with a cud of tobacco. "I'm Bonner. Got a place out there." He pointed in a southeasterly direction. "Raised these cattle myself." He pawed at the rain running down his face.

Travis eased away from them and rode gingerly around the small bunch; there were no more than twenty-five steers left. He was not familiar with brands, or the art of blotting, but he could recognize crude work when he saw it. Some wore Janeway's brand; the Circle T was now in a slightly altered form. There were several other brands which he suspected belonged to Janeway's friends.

Returning to Bonner, who sat his horse, suspicious and sullen, Travis said, "Naturally you include a bill of sale with the cattle to prove ownership."

"Never have before," Bonner said flatly. "See no need to now." He waved his hand and the other four men came over. "Sonny here don't think we own these steers."

They looked at each other and laughed, and Bonner stopped wiping his face long enough to bring a rifle from the saddle scabbard and mop water from the breech. This wasn't much of a threat by itself, but in light of what Travis had seen, it was strong enough.

"I'll tell you what I'm going to do," Jefferson Travis said. "I'm going to turn and ride back to the reservation building. And when I get there, Bonner, I'll expect you to come forward and present a bill of sale." He looked directly at the man, his expression flat, his smooth cheeks pulled tightly against the bones. "You know where you got the cattle, and I suspect I know too. But if you get the idea that a bullet in my back is going to solve anything, remember that I have fourteen men here who won't hesitate to kill you."

"What are you makin' such a fuss about?" Bonner demanded. "Jesus Christ, we've been sellin' cattle here for two years, and there ain't been any fuss." He pawed at his rain streaked face again. "All right, all right, we picked up the steers; they was strays. Now are you satisfied?"

"Branded strays, Bonner?" Travis wheeled his horse and rode back to the headquarters building. He saw Sergeant Ben Arness lounging there and snapped, "Mount the troop! You see those steers over there? I want them confiscated and driven back to Spanish

71

Spring."

This time Arness offered no argument. "Yes, sir," he said resignedly, and left the porch to call for Corporal Busik, who was in the stable with the detail.

Brewer, who had heard Travis' order, detached himself from his helpers. "What are you going to do? What was that you said, Mr. Travis?"

"Brewer, you know some of these cattle are stolen, don't you?"

"I don't know anything," Brewer said, "except that the Indians have to be given a beef ration and I can't afford to pay Dodge City prices, and that's what those bandits around Spanish Spring want for their steers." He took Travis by the arm and his voice took on a pleading tone. "I'm asking you to be reasonable, Mr. Travis. These Indians won't understand why you are impounding the cattle. What are you trying to do to me? Destroy me? Put an Indian uprising in my lap? In the name of heaven, man, these Indians have been getting free meat for so long they've lost the ambition to do for themselves. Once a month they get a steer, they expect a steer, and if they don't get it—"

"For God's sake, stop pulling at my sleeve!" Travis snapped. Brewer jerked his hands away as though the sleeve had suddenly turned hot. "Why do you assume that I'm picking on you, Mr. Brewer? I'm not blaming you for doing the best you can, but there has to be a line drawn somewhere." He reached out and tapped Brewer on the chest. "Buy all the stolen beef you want, but get a signed bill of sale. That way, if a cattleman complains, you've put yourself in the clear, and some rustler's neck in a rope."

"Well, I'll do it next time!" Brewer protested. "I've got almost thirty families here waiting for their beef issue and now you tell me you're confiscating the herd!" He put his hand to his face and it was trembling. "What am I to do, Mr. Travis? What am I going to do with these people?" His voice was edged with pain.

"I'm sorry, Mr. Brewer," Travis said, and remounted; his detail was forming in the muddy yard and the Indians were beginning to grumble because the rationing had stopped.

"Form on me, a line abreast," Travis said. "Carbines at the ready."

They came up on him, a perfect formation, and he walked them across the muddy interval to where Bonner and his men waited. When Travis was still fifty yards away, Bonner made his decision and bolted; the others followed him and Travis motioned for Arness and the others to round up the stock with the blotted brands.

He wheeled about and returned to headquarters, where half a hundred Indians stood in the rain, yelling, shaking their fists at Brewer, who was arguing with hysterical futility, his yammering drowned in the angry shouting of the crowd. When Travis pushed boldly through and gained the porch, Brewer turned on him. "There! Here's the man who took your cattle! Talk to *him!* Tell *him* about it!"

The Indians had a leader; he stepped forward and announced that he was named Limping Deer. Someone had once mentioned to Travis that the fury in an Indian's face always centered in the eyes; he saw now that this was true. The man looked like a bronze casting ready to be placed in the hallway of a public library, the image of savage pride trampled.

"I will speak for my people," Limping Deer said. "What right have you to steal our cattle? You stole our land, made war on us. Now we will not see our food

73

taken!" He waved his arms wildly. "All white men are liars, thieves! You will give us the cattle!"

"There will be more cattle," Travis said. "It will only be a few days, a week. You can wait. You won't starve."

"Limping Deer does not wait. He will have cattle today!"

"You will wait!" Travis said sternly. "I do not bargain with you, Limping Deer. It is the white man's law under which you must live, and it is my law you will obey now. These cattle are being returned to the men who own them. Other cattle will be brought to you. Now you will wait, and there will be no trouble over this!"

The Indian's face tightened while he raised his fist as though to strike. And suddenly Travis was mad with a blind anger at the whole impossibly tangled mess. He grabbed the Indian's wrist, twisted painfully, and threw him flat on his back. His voice was filled with fury as he said, "Now you listen to me, you stinking savage! You camp on the agency door so you won't miss anything that's free, but you earn none of it! You want the agent to feed you, to take care of you, and when he does not, you curse him! Now the United States Army has spoken and if you have any brains in your head you'll listen carefully! You take your shouting friends and go to your homes, and when more cattle come, you'll get them!" All the time he talked he kept his knee pressed against Limping Deer's throat, disgracing him before his people, humbling him as he had never been humbled before. Then Travis released him and turned his back on him. He took Brewer by the arm and pulled him to one side. "Now get this straight, Mr. Brewer, I'm going to Spanish Spring to talk to the cattlemen about a fair price for their beef, a price that you should pay." Brewer opened his mouth to say something, but Travis cut him off. "I'm going to find out how much a steer will bring in Dodge City, and how much it costs to drive there. That amount I think should be deducted by the cattlemen when they sell here. Now before you start crying that it's too high, it might pay you to remember that it won't be so easy to put leftover dollars in your pocket as it used to be. Good day, Mr. Brewer. I'll see you in about a week."

He turned away from the man, stepped off the porch and rammed his way through the angry Indians and went into the saddle. Without a backward look, he rode off in the pouring rain to catch up with his detail and the recovered cattle, now a mile away from the reservation.

6

THE DETAIL TRAVELED SOUTHEASTWARD IN THE slanting rain, pushing the small herd before them. In an hour the gray smudge of sky blotted out the reservation buildings, wiped them away as though erased from a blackboard. Even with the ponchos it was impossible to keep dry. Campaign hats funneled water down collars, and before they had traveled five miles, each man rode a soggy saddle and longed for a scorching sun to dry him out.

This came in the afternoon, when the clouds parted and steam began to rise from the sodden earth. There was considerable water running off; each depression held a rushing, muddy torrent, and the buffalo wallows filled rapidly.

Since the fight, Ben Arness had not spoken to Travis except when he had to, and on the march back he traded places with Corporal Busik, who now sided Travis at the head of the detail. Busik was a dark-complected man, a career soldier who did what he was told and never asked questions. He had a melon-shaped face and thick lips, and constantly chewed cut-plug tobacco.

Now he said conversationally, "In another twenty days, sir, the buffalo will be migrating. They move north and south every year, spring and fall." He made a sweeping gesture with his hand to include the whole prairie. "This time next week you'll see buffalo hunter camps all over. You think the slaughter at the agency was something, wait 'til you see the buffalo hunt. The prairie takes on a horrible stink; the hunters just take the hides and leave the carcasses to rot. The Indians go a little crazy then; they believe it's a sin to waste anything, even the bones. They hate the hunters and the hunters hate the Indians. You can smell trouble in the air like woodsmoke." He took off his hat and wiped his forehead, then put it back on again. "The Indians make war talk and the drums go all night and they put on paint, but what can they do? They know how far a buffalo rifle will shoot and that six hunters, holed up in a wallow, can hold off a hundred Indians. But a few always break away from the reservation and try their luck, sir. And they get killed and everyone raises hell. But how can you stop 'em?"

Jefferson Travis considered this for a while, then said, "When the hunters start killing buffalo, corporal, we'll be around."

Busik shrugged his heavy shoulders. "You can't stop much with fourteen men, sir."

"No, I suppose not, but we're going to try this year."

The cattle were turned into the barracks compound and a two-man guard was placed over them. Two more troopers were dispatched to notify the cattlemen and General Thomas C. Wrigley; Travis felt certain that the general would want to attend the meeting if only to defend the rights of his homesteaders.

With a few hours to kill before his invited guests gathered, Travis had his bath and shave and changed into clean clothes. He walked to the express office to see if any dispatches had arrived for him; there were none, and he was vastly relieved, for the best news right now was no news at all. When Major Deacon received all the threatened complaints about his new officer, he would be foaming at the mouth and penning a bitter letter, and Travis figured that until he saw it he could carry on in his own way, as he saw fit.

Janeway arrived first and came directly to Travis' office. He tied his horse in front and came across the porch, pausing in the open doorway. The daylight was fading and Travis was lighting the lamp; without turning to see who it was, he said, "Come in and sit down."

"Thank you," Janeway said. He unbuttoned his coat and shifted his pistol holster around to a more comfortable position. Travis looked at him for a moment and then Janeway said, "I guess I owe you an apology, lieutenant."

"You don't owe me a thing, Mr. Janeway," Travis said. "Where are your friends?"

"One of your soldiers stopped at my place and I came right on in," he said. "The others will be along. How many head did you save?"

"Twenty-five. The Indians got at least that many more."

"You haven't told me yet who was selling my cattle."

"No, I haven't," Travis said softly. "And all the steers aren't yours. There are other brands mixed in."

"Let's not split hairs—" He craned his neck and looked out the door as General Wrigley drove into the yard. "That's all we need, an unreconstructed Rebel. How the devil did he get wind of this?"

"I invited him," Travis said, and went out to greet Wrigley. "Come on inside, general. You're early, but I imagine we can find some way to pass the time."

Wrigley was in a peckish humor; he grunted something unintelligible to Travis and stomped inside. Then he saw Janeway sitting there and his mustache bristled as his lips settled in a disapproving line.

"I can wait outside," Wrigley snapped.

"Never mind," Janeway said, rising. "*I'll* wait

78

outside."

"Why don't you both sit down?" Travis asked. "After all, you're here about a problem that concerns us all."

They sat down, on opposite sides of the room. Travis lit a cigar and studied them briefly. Wrigley kept fidgeting with his gold watch chain and casting oblique glances at Janeway, who crossed one leg over the other and studied the stitching in his boots.

Finally Wrigley said, "You have a gall, lieutenant, taking over those steers in such a peremptory manner."

"There was a question of ownership to be settled," Travis said, smiling. "If I'm satisfied that the homesteaders came into those steers honestly, I'll see that they're returned."

"They were rustled and you know it," Janeway snapped.

"He doesn't know any such thing!" Wrigley countered flatly.

"All right, all right, we'll save the bickering until the others get here," Travis said, and went on puffing on his cigar. He was beginning to develop a taste for tobacco; the first few cigars he had smoked had been for appearance. A cigar always made a man seem older, gave him a touch of maturity.

Hodges, Rider, and Butram arrived together; they tied their horses and came on in, smiling. This faded a little when they saw Wrigley sitting there. At Travis' invitation they sat down.

"I think we can begin now," Travis said.

"Where's Ben Arness?" Wrigley asked.

"The sergeant no longer dictates army policy in this district," Travis said. "He's where he belongs, with the enlisted men." Then he looked at each of them. "Gentlemen, I have under guard twenty-five steers.

Eleven of them carry the Circle T; I believe that's your brand, Mr. Janeway." He consulted a sheet of paper. "Six are branded S on a Rail."

"That's mine," Hodges said.

"Three are Double O Bar."

"Mine," Rider said.

"The other five are Rocking Chair."

"That's me," Butram said. He looked at Wrigley and laughed. "Your damned thievin' bunch didn't get away with it this time, did they?"

"All right!" Travis said harshly as Wrigley started to rise. "General, the men who had possession of those steers claimed they found them on the prairie. Do you have anything to say about that?"

"If they said that, then it's so."

"They're lying," Rider said. "I keep closer tabs on my stock than that." He looked at Travis. "You haven't told us the names of the men who had them."

"I don't intend to," Travis said smoothly. "Gentlemen, let's be realistic about this. If I told you who they were, I'd find them hanging from a tree or a barn rafter. Right?"

"Naturally!" Butram snapped.

"That's why I won't say," Travis told them.

"I thought you were on our side," Janeway said sullenly. "God damn it, I almost apologized too."

"Just a moment!" Travis snapped. "Gentlemen, we're going to reach an agreement before we break up this meeting. Now you cattlemen have been holding out for high prices, and the agent can't stretch his budget that far. You have no call to charge a Dodge City price for your steers and get fat on the excess profit."

"We've got to charge high to make up for the rustling losses," Janeway said. "You get Wrigley and his crooked friends to stop putting their ropes on our steers and we'll meet the agent and establish a fair price."

"I'm sure the general will agree to that," Travis said, then looked at Wrigley.

"You're trying to chivvy me into a position that will suit you," Wrigley said angrily. "I'll agree to nothing."

Travis thought this over for a moment, then said, "General, I'm going to write a report tonight on this meeting, and I wouldn't like to have to say that you were uncooperative. I know your friends have to eat, and they steal a few steers to tide them over, but it all counts up, sir, and the cattlemen feel the pinch."

"Amen to that," Rider said. "Keep talkin' there, sonny."

"General," Travis said, "I find your attitude very unrealistic, in the face of a possible solution."

"What solution? You're discriminating against the homesteaders."

"Being poor, sir, does not entitle a man to steal." Travis slapped his hand on the desk. "I'm not going to mince words with you, general. I seek a solution to this, a just solution for the cattlemen, who have been rustled in the past, and a solution for the Indian agent, who must either pay high prices or buy stolen beef, and some just solution to the problems of your friends. Now, I've reached the cattlemen if I can put a halt to the rustling. You can help there. A word from you would do more than six companies of cavalry."

"Provided I gave that word," Wrigley said.

"I think you will, sir."

The general's eyebrow raised. "Will I?" He laughed cynically. "You're not only young, but foolish."

"General, unless you give it, I'll reveal the names of the men who were selling the steers. I venture to say

81

they'll all be hanged within twenty-four hours." His glance touched the cattlemen. "Right, gentlemen?"

"Right!" they said in unison.

Wrigley's complexion faded. "You *wouldn't* do that! They'd blame me!"

"Only if you force me, general. Make no mistake, sir. I'm dead serious. And I won't give you long to make up your mind."

"It would cost you your commission, Mr. Travis."

"I'm not so sure of that. After all, it really is my *duty* to report their names."

"This is dirty blackmail," Wrigley said "That's all it is. You've sold out to the cattlemen." He shook his head sadly. "All right, Mr. Travis. I'll do what I can."

"We are assuming," Travis said, "that it will be enough." He turned to Janeway. "I promised the agent some cattle. You'll have to drive a herd of about fifty right away."

"Are you running my business?"

Travis shook his head. "No, but I don't want Indian trouble and neither do you. As for your price, I believe the costs of a drive to Dodge should be deducted. The agent feels this is fair, and so do I."

Janeway stared at him for a moment, then shook his head and laughed. "Sonny, you beat the hell out of anything I ever saw. All right, since you've gone to so much trouble and brought some of our stolen stock back, we'll agree." He motioned to the others. "I speak for all."

"Then, I believe the entire matter is settled," Travis said. "General, would you remain?"

The others filed out, mounted, and rode away. Wrigley looked at Travis for a moment, then said, "What could we possibly have to say to each other now, sir?"

"I don't enjoy the plight of your homesteaders," Travis said. "What I've seen of them, they're hog dirty and mouse poor. Isn't there anything that can be done for them? And I don't mean stealing army horses or Janeway's cattle."

Wrigley shook his head. "It's hard to get started when you have nothing."

"You look prosperous enough, general."

"Meaning?"

"That you're not leasing that land from the goodness of your heart," Travis said. "The Indian agent showed me a map giving the location of every settler. I counted sixty-seven, all in my district. What do they pay you for a sublease?" He saw stubbornness come into Wrigley's eyes, and added, "I suppose I could get a court order to look at your books, general."

"That isn't necessary," Wrigley said. "They pay me two hundred and fifty dollars on signing, and a hundred dollars a year."

"Let's see now—that's roughly sixteen thousand dollars, and sixty-seven hundred dollars a year. Not bad. I don't think a United States Senator makes much more than that. It isn't difficult now to understand why you want these people to survive on the prairie. If they don't raise the lease money, they're out." He shrugged. "But I suppose that in itself isn't much of a tragedy. When one leaves, you can always release the property, another two hundred and fifty, and a hundred a year. I don't see how you can lose."

Wrigley stared at Jefferson Travis. "You make it sound cold and mercenary, Mr. Travis."

"Well it is, isn't it?"

"It's a legitimate business, sir. Good night."

He went outside and got into his buggy, and after he wheeled out of the yard Travis left his office and walked the few blocks to Doctor Summer's house to have his arm dressed. It itched considerably, which indicated that it was healing well.

Hope Randall was sitting on the front porch, shelling peas, when he came up the walk. A shaft of lamplight filtering through the front screen door cast its golden glow about her. She lifted her head as he approached.

"My mother used to give me a nickel a gallon for that kind of work," Travis, said.

"I pay off in gingersnaps. Sit down."

"Could I get the doctor to put a new dressing on my arm?"

"I'll do that," she said, and put the pan aside. She led the way into Summers' office and motioned for him to sit down. He rolled up his sleeve and she got out the salve and dressing. When she cut the old bandage away, she looked carefully at the wound. "It's healing very well. In another week it ought to close up."

"Well, it hasn't bothered me at all."

She gave him an amused look. "Jeff, I don't think anything really bothers you. You're one of those rare, self-sufficient men who never seems to need help with anything."

"Except myself." He smiled. "I just came from a meeting." He told her about it as she wrapped his arm and tied the bandage.

"Wrigley gave in? I've never heard of him doing a thing like that before."

"He wants to pretend that I didn't give him any choice," Travis said. "But it's not that, Hope. He just doesn't want to lose money."

"Is it wrong to want money?"

"Guess not," he said. "Of course, I've never had any, so I wouldn't know. Do you know how much a lieutenant makes a month?"

"Yes, but they seem to get along on it, don't they?"

"If they go light on whiskey and cards." He rolled his sleeve down. "I'll help you shell those peas. Anything for an excuse to sit and talk and look at you."

"It's dark on the porch."

He smiled. "Don't worry. I know what you look like; a little darkness won't make me forget. Hope, I—"

"Let's shell the peas," she said, and went outside.

He took a pan and sat on the steps near her feet, cracking husks and stripping peas into another small pan. "Do you feel a compulsion to do the right thing, Hope?"

"No. I don't worry about my mistakes. You shouldn't either."

"I've got a report to write," he said. "Should I confess all, how I maneuvered the general into doing what I wanted?"

She laughed. "Only fools confess all. Jeff, are you still trying to find the right and wrong of everything?"

"I suppose. But who is wrong?"

"All of us. We're all a little right too. Jeff, the Indians are right; they've been cheated and lied to all down the line. And the buffalo hunters are right; they're making money and spending it and towns are being built and railroads. The homesteaders are poor, but some make it and they're people; people are important to the land. And Janeway's got a point when he says that he was here first and the politicians sold him short when they gave the waterholes to farmers. I think the homesteaders are more deserving, but then, ask anyone in Spanish Spring and I'm afraid you'll get four opinions." She set her pan aside.

"I'm beginning to see," he said, "Just why Major Deacon likes a neutral policy. It's not easy to takes sides." He looked at her. "Do you still think I will?"

"I still think you must, sooner or later, Jeff." She patted his arm and then let her hand rest there. "You're a very straitlaced man. By that I mean, you have a firm, almost profound sense of morality. And it's somehow misplaced out here." She frowned. "Do you see what I mean?" You want to apply this severe sense of justice that governs you to the homesteaders who don't understand it, and to the Indians who don't want it really, and to Janeway who would think it so much nonsense."

"Do you think it is, Hope?"

"No," she said softly. "I like it."

"Hope, did a man ever kiss you on the front porch?"

"Good heavens, no!"

"I am about to," Jefferson Travis said, and without giving her time to protest, he pulled her into his arms and pressed his lips on hers. He was surprised at the warmth of her, the fragileness, and strength.

When he released her, he said quietly, "I'm not going to apologize."

Doctor Summers, who was coming up the dark path, heard him and said, "I wouldn't either, Mr. Travis. And I hope you're not blushing." He took his bag into the house and came back out. "Any man who pursues such a bold course will be a general someday."

"Really, Doctor, I'm a man of sincere intentions and—"

"Will you stop explaining?" Summers asked. "Do you want to ruin it? I don't understand you young people, always explaining yourselves as though you

86

were afraid someone wouldn't take you right."

"Doctor," Hope said, "why don't you wash for supper?"

"What? Oh!" He chuckled. "I never seem to know when I'm not wanted. Well, young man, come to supper sometime this week, if you haven't already been asked." He went into the house, humming to himself.

"I want to talk to you about something," Hope Randall said.

"About the kiss?"

She nodded. "If you were just trying to prove to yourself that you were a man, I'm going to be angry."

"It wasn't that at all," he said sincerely. "Hope, you're a chatterbox most of the time, but I like to listen to you. I think I'm falling in love with you. Do you mind?"

"No, I don't mind at all. Do you want to stay for supper?"

"Can't. I have to write that report."

"Be a little kinder to yourself, Jeff. Do you know what I mean?"

"Yes, but I have to be as honest about myself as with others," he said, then kissed her lightly and walked back to the barracks.

General Wrigley found Sergeant Ben Arness in the saloon, nursing a glass of whiskey. He sided Arness, wiggled his finger at the bartender for a good bottle, then took the sergeant to an isolated table. Business was light at this hour; there were a few men playing cards and a drunk sleeping it off in the corner.

Wrigley said, "I can't get used to dealing with that pink-faced kid instead of you, Ben. Somehow I just can't get along with him."

"Who can? I'm down on him. So's every man in the detail."

"Is that a fact? He must be a real son-of-a-bitch to get along with." He refilled Arness' glass. Almost on cue, Owen Gates came in, a toothpick probing the crevices between his teeth. He came over to their table and sat down.

"You're looking mighty glum, Ben," Gates said.

"Ben's getting a crawful of that kid lieutenant," Wrigley said. "You can't blame him, Owen. It's kids like him that give the army a bad name; always meddling, always stirring things up."

Arness squinted and shook his finger. "He just ain't army, general. You got to learn to soldier and it takes years. Why, I'll bet half of the men are ready to go over the hill right now. You know, he's been on patrol damned near ever since he got here?"

"I'd get out," Owen Gates said.

"After twenty-seven years?" Wrigley asked. "That's foolish, sheriff. Besides, if Ben retired now, half of the men would go with him."

"Yeah, I never thought of that," Gates said. "But you'll never trim him down to size as long as you're in the army, Ben." He tapped his shoulders. "Those little gold threads sewn there will beat you every time."

"Why don't you come and work for me?" Wrigley asked. "A hundred a month and the authority to back you up."

Arness looked at him. "What kind of authority?"

"Gates' badge," Wrigley said flatly. "Owen's going to give it up and I need a capable man in his place, a man I can trust, a man who sees my side. You know I'm in the right, Ben."

"You and Grace Beaumont could get married, Ben,"

Gates said. "It's what she wants, you know that." He thumped Ben Arness on the arm. "And then you can take a crack at that lieutenant, Ben, and the army can't do a thing about it."

"Think it over," Wrigley said. "Here, take the bottle with you, Ben. You let me know tomorrow, won't you?"

Arness nodded and stood up, the bottle under his arm. He walked unsteadily toward the swinging doors and then on down the street.

"Well?" Gates said. "What do you think?"

"He hates officers, and he loves authority," Wrigley said. "And then there's the woman pulling at him. That's something in our favor."

"Yes," Gates said wistfully. "But to give it all up after twenty-seven years—"

"I don't give a damn if he's got fifty years in the army," Wrigley said. "When I need a man, I need him, and that's all I think about." He turned in his chair and snapped his fingers for the bartender to bring him another bottle.

7

"IT'S FOR BEN'S OWN GOOD," OWEN GATES SAID. HE was standing in Grace Beaumont's doorway, hat in hand. The parlor lamp was turned up brightly, for she had been sewing; his knock had interrupted her. "Ben's at the barracks, Mrs. Beaumont. You want I should send him around?"

"I suppose," she said doubtfully. "It *is* for Ben's good, isn't it?" Then she sighed. "He's going to feel lost for a while. But he had to get out sometime. Thank you for coming around, Owen."

"Glad to do it," he said.

He left her house and walked to the barracks grounds. There was a lamp burning in Lieutenant Travis' office, and Gates knocked politely although the door was open. Travis put aside the letter he had been writing.

"What is it, sheriff?"

"Thought I'd better ask your permission first," Gates said, "but Mrs. Beaumont would like to see Ben Arness. Just thought I'd let him know."

"He isn't very sober," Travis said. Then he nodded toward the end where the enlisted men slept. "But go ahead. It's none of my business."

Gates turned to the door, then hesitated. He smiled pleasantly. "Making out your report card, lieutenant?"

"Yes, and I'm putting you down for a failure in effort."

Gates looked amused. "The general gave me my orders before you came, and he'll be giving them after you leave, which should be soon. It's too bad you have to find an answer for everything. Can't you just let things work themselves out?" He jammed his hands into his pockets. "But it's no use giving you advice. You go ahead and do what you have to do, sonny. It'll be a relief to all of us to see you leave."

Travis stared out the door after Gates left, then went on to finish the letter he was writing to his brother. He wanted to straighten him out on a lot of things, such as his notion that the west was a place where a man did what he wanted to do, and where he could pick up a fortune without raising a sweat. Travis wanted to assure him that it wasn't much different from back home, where everyone worked toward his own small dream, and if a man somehow got crowded out, no one really cared. He would have liked to write about his work, convincing them that it was important, but he couldn't very well boast about recovering two strayed army horses and twenty-five stolen cattle, and angering a lot of people in the process. Written down, that wouldn't sound very important at all, and Travis wondered if he could bring it into a truer perspective by going into detail about the geographic and economic structure of the country. He felt powerless to explain how important one poor homesteader became when the permanent population was less than ten per thousand square miles. And his brother would think the furor over a few horses ridiculous, for he had never owned one. He would find it hard to believe that the loss of a horse could cost a man his life on the plains. Each morning Paul got up and walked five blocks to work, his tin lunch pail in hand. And each evening he walked home. Now and then, when he wanted to go to Utica, a distance of twelve miles, he would take the train and stay overnight to rest up from the trip.

No, he wouldn't understand at all about towns being

three to five days' ride from each other. So Jefferson Travis wrote about the Indians being troublesome by nature, and the settlers being inclined to thievery, and the cattlemen being prone to take the law into their own hands. He knew that Paul would believe these things, for they dovetailed so neatly with his own opinions: that the uneducated couldn't be trusted, the poor were all thieves, and the rich were always overbearing.

Since Sergeant Arness was away from the barracks, Travis went to see Corporal Busik. "General march order at dawn," Travis said. "Three weeks' rations; that'll mean pack horses. And double ammunition rations."

"Yes, sir," Busik said. "Shall I relay that to the sergeant when he comes back?"

"Yes, corporal," Travis said, "but I believe I'm capable of running this detail without Sergeant Arness."

Busik grinned. "Yes, sir, we've noticed that. Meaning no disrespect, sir, but we all put you down for a tough time at first. Not that any of us have it in for second lieutenants, sir, but generally they're long on regulations and short on horse sense."

"Thank you, corporal. I consider that a compliment."

Busik went back to his quarters and Travis turned in for the night, feeling warmed by the corporal's expression of confidence. *Someday,* he thought, *I may make a passable first lieutenant.*

He woke very early, breakfasted, and started packing his saddlebags. Sergeant Arness came to his room and knocked; Travis turned and saw him, then motioned him in.

"I'd like to have a word with you, sir," Arness said.

"All right. I hope we can bury the hatchet, sergeant."

"I don't change my mind easily, sir." He wiped a

hand across his mouth. "If it's all the same with you, I'd like for you to write a letter for me." He waited a moment as though he wanted Travis to ask what about, and when the lieutenant said nothing, Arness said, "I want to retire, sir. Effective immediately."

Jefferson Travis sat down on his bunk, genuinely disturbed. "You want to throw away twenty-seven years, sergeant? Because of me? In the name of heaven, man, I'd rather transfer myself first." He spread his hands in an appeal. "Sergeant, this isn't a matter of who's right or wrong, or how you feel about officers. Twenty-seven years of service! A man just doesn't up and throw it—"

"Will you write the letter for me, sir? I want to be relieved immediately."

Travis sighed. "I don't suppose there's anything I can say that would—"

"No, sir. My mind's made up." He jammed his hands into his pockets. "I've got a job right here in Spanish Spring; I don't need the army anymore."

"Very well, sergeant. I'll write the letter, but you understand that it will require Major Deacon's endorsement and it won't go out on the stage for another five days."

"That's all right," Arness said. "You just write the letter." He saluted stiffly and went out, and a few minutes later Corporal Busik came to the office, greatly agitated. "Ben s packing his gear, says he's getting out. Is that true, sir?"

"You should be pleased, Busik. It's another stripe for you."

"Hang the stripe!" He shook his head. "God knows Arness has been hell to live with sometimes, but with three more years to go, and a top soldier's hooks just around the corner—"

"He made up his own mind," Travis said. "I'll endorse a letter promoting you to sergeant. Pick a good man to promote to corporal.'

"Trooper Ardmore, sir. He's reliable and he's army. Sixteen years in dirty-shirt blue."

"All right," Travis said.

He was a little crowded for time, with these letters to write, but he managed it and didn't hold up the detail to do it. Ben Arness' resignation had to be in triplicate, and there was a place for him to sign all three copies. The order promoting Busik and Ardmore was a simple letter; Travis intended to forward all of them when he returned.

With the detail mounted and putting Spanish Spring behind them, Travis felt that everything was all out of kilter without Arness riding behind him, with his ingrained prejudices and stony expression. This was his first awareness that it could actually be comforting to be disliked by someone.

At the crossing he noted that Regan's place was still locked up; the man must be on a drunk at Fort Dodge, he had had time to return by now. They stopped for a ten-minute rest, then went on, riding north toward the wide scatter of homesteader soddies.

Around noon they approached a place built of earth and sunk well into the ground, both for convenience of construction and safety from the twisters that now and then ripped through. A pack of naked children were gathering buffalo chips as the patrol drew near, then they ran for the soddy and an Indian woman came to the doorway to see what had disturbed them.

A man came out, armed with a repeating rifle, and Travis recognized him as Bonner, the man he had relieved of the stolen cattle. He wore a buckskin shirt over filthy long underwear, and he was barefoot.

"Guess you've come to arrest me now," he said, putting up his rifle. "I can't fight you all."

"You're not under arrest," Travis said. "We'd like to fill our canteens from your spring." Bonner waved permission and Ardmore went around and gathered them up.

"Ain't been sleepin' much since I came back from the reservation," Bonner said. "Been expectin' to be hung."

"By cattlemen?" Travis shook his head. "They don't know who was selling their steers."

From Bonner's expression, Travis could see that he wanted to believe this, but didn't dare. "You wouldn't lie to me, would you, lieutenant?"

"Why should I?"

"Because I'm nuthin'. Most people don't reckon me worth wastin' the truth on." He laughed without humor. "Sonny, you don't know what it is to be nuthin'. Was I hung, it wouldn't mean anything to the men on the other end of the rope. My kind is just thrown away."

"Not by me," Travis said. "Bonner, I think I kept you from being hanged sooner or later; you're not smart enough to steal for long and get away with it." Ardmore came back with the filled canteens and passed them around before mounting. "Keep your rope off branded steers, Bonner."

"I surely will," Bonner said. "And much obliged for the favor."

Travis led them away from the soddy, cutting toward the Dodge City trail, an ill-defined, faint wearing in the grass, a jagged scar left on the earth by wagons. It ran in a faint curve, out of the vast flatlands to the south into the monotonous expanse to the north, where the horizon

95

melted into the earth in a bluish mist and one could not be separated from the other.

The air was dry and oven hot, yet there was an unusual charge of electricity in everything; it set up static in the clothing when the seat of the britches rubbed the saddle. Near sundown, a purple-gray haze swallowed the sun, and not a breath of wind stirred.

Sergeant Busik sided Travis and spoke in a hushed voice. "I don't like this, sir. Look at the color of that sky. Like old lead." He jerked his head toward the column. "The animals are getting spooky too."

"What do you think is causing it? A storm coming?"

"Yeah, but a storm like you never seen before, sir. Winds strong enough to knock a horse down, carry him off even. We call it a twister, sir. She'll likely build all night, and tomorrow, when it gets hot, she'll let go." He waved his hand toward the distant horizon. "The sky turns black and a whirling cloud comes across the prairie, sir, like a funnel spinning on its end. It uproots trees, buildings, and everything in its path."

"Where's the nearest timber?" Travis asked.

Busik scratched his head. "Ash Creek, I guess. About four hours ride from here."

"Forced march?"

"No, sir. That way you could cut it to two and a half."

"All right, Busik. Lead out."

They made only short stops, alternating the trot with the walk, and arrived at Ash Creek well after dark. There were some trees on each side of the creek, and this slash in the earth's face was almost narrow enough to jump a horse across.

Travis dismounted the detail, had the horses picketed, and ordered Busik to have the hatchets broken out. He wanted trees felled across the creek to form a large shelter, and while six men chopped, others rigged rope harness and began to haul the downed timber into place.

They worked the night through, overlaying the logs with brush, then fresh earth, until they were heavily covered. It was an ideal spot for shelter, for the creek contained no water, just four inches of drying mud in the bottom.

Beneath the cover of logs and brush and earth, Travis ordered camp made and the horses brought in. He was on watch when daylight came, the most frightening dawn he had ever seen. The sky was like slate, and it was a chore to breathe the hot, humid air: To the southwest the sky was the color of oil smoke on a lamp chimney.

Suddenly a wind woke across the flats, husking dust before it, driving stinging particles of dirt against Travis' face. Busik came to stand beside him and said, "She's a twister, sir. Pretty soon you'll see her, like a black whirling funnel. No tellin' where she'll hit or what her path will be. A man can only take cover and hope it's good enough."

Finally the leaden sky took on motion, a whirling torrent of lifted dust, and ferocious winds, running crookedly toward the ground, swelling, nearing. The wind increased to awesome proportions, a solid bursting roar of sound, and the earth seemed to tremble beneath their feet. For an hour it ripped its devastation across the prairie, the main funnel passing east of Travis' position, yet the force of the wind was enough to spin dirt and brush from the roof of his makeshift shelter. One or two logs were displaced and fell, but no one was injured. He watched the course of the twister and wondered how close it had come to Spanish Spring; it had seemed to come from that direction.

They did not leave the creek bed until late morning, when the wind had died and the twister was long gone. The air was still full of dust, blotting the sun from the sky as Travis mounted his detail; they were all tired from the night's hard work and the tension of waiting out the storm.

To Busik, Travis said, "Tell the men I'm sorry all the work was for nothing."

"They didn't mind, sir," Busik said.

"We'll push northeast and follow the twister's path," Travis said. "If anyone was in the way of it, they'll likely need help."

"If they were in the way, sir, they'll be beyond help."

"Nevertheless, we'll take a look," Travis said firmly.

He wished that he had a more detailed map, one marked with the location of the settlers. After seeing Brewer's wall map, Travis carried a section chart and meant to record this information the next time he touched agency headquarters.

Toward noon of a scalding day they rested in a buffalo wallow; it had six inches of mud in the center, so they squatted below the rim and ate cold rations. Sergeant Busik hunkered down near Travis to talk.

"I know of six or seven families who could have been caught in this thing," Busik said. He looked at the sky and the forming clouds. "Wouldn't surprise me if we got rain this evening, sir."

"We can stand something to break this heat," Travis said. "We'll rest here until the sun goes down. Tell everyone to get what sleep they can."

"No need to tell 'em that, sir," Busik said. He nodded and Travis looked; three of the men were already snoring.

Travis lay back with a handkerchief folded over his

eyes and got some sleep; a cool wind woke him in total darkness and he sat up. Busik was near by and a touch brought him awake.

"We'd better be moving," Travis said.

A bright stab of lightning illuminated the prairie, and an instant later a thunderclap bounded across the sky. "Hope it comes down good," Busik said, and went to stir the others.

They were moving by the time the pelting rain began to fall, and they walked their horses, letting it beat against their ponchos and wash down their faces. Some time later they saw a blossom of yellow lamplight in the distance and rode toward it.

A barking dog ventured out, snapping at the horses' heels, and one of the troopers shied him away with a whipped rope end. A man, was walking around his scattered soddy, carrying a lantern, his clothes soaked to the skin. He held the lantern high when Travis dismounted and walked up to him.

"You got hit bad," Travis said. "Anyone hurt?"

The man shook his head. "I live here alone." He peered at the soldiers. "I'm all right. Just digging out. Better go on north to the Pearl's place. They was likely in the path of it too."

Travis turned to his horse. "What's your name, in case they ask about you?"

"Riscoe. Say, you fellas wouldn't have some coffee to spare, would you? Found my pot, and there's no hole in it."

"Busik, fix him up with some bacon, flour, coffee and sugar. Better give him some dried beans too."

This was more than Riscoe had hoped for, and he said, "By golly, that's mighty decent of you. I guess I'm goin' to stay alive after all."

The way he said it, with an almost prayerful thankfulness, made Travis realize anew how thinly these people clung to the line of life. The twister had ripped up his buildings and killed his livestock; he had nothing left but his life, and Travis' native generosity had just renewed the lease on it.

"How far is it to the Pearls'?" Travis asked.

"Oh, sixteen miles or so," Riscoe said. "Say my howdy to 'em."

"We'll do that," Travis said and stepped into the saddle. The leather felt hard and uncomfortable and his leg muscles ached, yet he turned his detail out of the yard.

He had to conserve the horses so he kept them at a slow walk, and dismounted often to save them. The rain turned to a steady drizzle and the soft ground made walking a misery, yet they kept going, their boots sucking at the mud. Travis figured, that he could spare the horses until he made his swing around to the reservation; two days there on stable feed would put life back into them.

They wore out a miserable night and when dawn came the drizzle slackened to a stinging mist, pushed by a sharp, thrusting wind. Through the gray light they could make out the rubble of buildings and a lean-to barn, and Travis decided this must be the Pearls' place.

When they rode into the yard and dismounted, Pearl came out, flanked by his strapping sons. He was a giant of a man, six foot four in his moccasins, and his chest was like the bole of an old tree, thick and immensely strong.

"Are you Mr. Pearl?" Travis asked

"I be," he said. Then he looked at the tired troopers. "I thought the twister cleaned off the prairie. Where was you hidin'?"

"In a creek bed," Travis said. "It passed us by. Anyone hurt here?"

Pearl's face settled into sadness. "My girl, Nan." He pointed to a mound of fresh earth to one side of what had been his soddy. "We just finished the buryin'. Be you goin' near the reservation, you tell Brewer." He saw Travis' puzzlement, and added, "Brewer's stopped here a number of times, and he always looked on my little girl with a gentleman's favor. She never knew much politeness in her life, young fella, and she thought Brewer was somethin' special." His voice grew soft. "I guess he was, 'cause he saw woman in her, which pleased her. She was goin' to be eighteen come green up."

"I'm sorry," Travis said sincerely. "Is there anything I can do?"

The older boy's name was Kyle. He said, "Mister, you got a Bible?"

"I haven't, I'm sorry," Travis said.

Kyle shook his head, as though he hadn't really expected one. "I wanted somethin' said over her, that's all. She knew only good thoughts, mister. Nary a word of meanness passed her lips, and bein' poor never bothered her much, never made her bitter toward no one."

Travis said softly, "Gentlemen, I believe I can quote a proper scripture from memory, if you'll permit me."

Pearl said, "We'd be in your debt."

Turning to Busik, Travis meant to give an order, but the man was already turning to the troopers. "Column of twos!" he said. "Dress it up there! Are you Tennessee farmers?" Then he pivoted and saluted. "Detail formed, sir."

"Thank you, sergeant."

They walked to the fresh mound and Travis stood at the head, with the Pearls about him, flanked by grimy, rain-soaked soldiers, all at attention, unmindful of the drizzle.

"Uncover," Travis said, and they were precise about at the earth which covered a girl he had never seen. "I have never spoken at a graveside before; perhaps there are passages more suitable than the one I recall. According to Matthew, Christ went up into a mountain, and when his disciples came to him, and the multitudes gathered around, he spoke to them, saying: 'Blessed are the poor in spirit, for theirs is the kingdom of heaven. Blessed are they which do hunger and thirst after righteousness; for they shall be filled. Blessed are the meek; for they shall inherit the earth. Blessed are the pure in heart; for they shall see God.' Amen." He glanced at his men. "Cover. Sergeant Busik, mount the detail."

"Yes, sir. All right, you heard Mr. Travis."

Pearl was wiping his nose with the back of his hand. "That was mighty nice, mister."

"It seems so little to do, Mr. Pearl. If you need provisions—"

"No, no, we'll manage. Lost my wife two years ago. Bull buffalo got her, just over yonder." He pointed, then rubbed his huge, hairy forearms. "My little Nan couldn't read a word or sign her name, but she knew about God and them things, mister. Some people just know, 'cause they're born gentle."

"Yes," Travis said. "I had almost forgotten there was such a thing out here." He turned quickly to his horse and went into the saddle. A wave of his hand got them going and he turned in the direction of the Indian

102

reservation.

Busik rode a pace behind Travis, and the young man turned and looked at him before speaking. "These settlers—" he hesitated, "Damn it, Busik, how many starts does a man have to make in one lifetime?"

"Some never stop making them, sir. And it's a damned shame that they should have to, sir."

They rode on in silence and finally the rain stopped.

8

ON THE WAY TO THE RESERVATION, TRAVIS BEGAN TO get a true picture of the twister's devastating effect; it had disturbed and littered a twenty-mile swath, uprooting the brush. When he drew in sight of the agency buildings and Indian camp, he saw damage there; roofs were torn off, lodges were down and scattered, and the horse corral was partially wrecked. He realized that their hastily made shelter had protected them only because they had been on the fringe of the twister's path, as had the agency, yet the winds had been forceful enough to cause damage.

When he dismounted, he gave Busik his orders. "Turn the mounts into the corral, then take a detail and make some emergency repairs. See what you can do to help straighten this up a little."

"Yes, sir."

"We'll remain here for a few days," Travis said. Then he walked on to the headquarters building, where he met Brewer in the door.

"That was a real wind," Brewer said. "We didn't catch the full brunt of it though. Where were you?"

"In a creek bed," Travis said. He took Brewer's arm and led him inside. "We just came from the Pearls' place, Mr. Brewer. I'm sorry to have to tell you that Nan is dead."

Brewer looked at him for a moment, then he turned abruptly to the liquor cabinet, poured himself a drink and sat down.

"It's hard to believe," he said softly, and drained his glass; he refilled it immediately.

Travis cleared his throat, "We gave her a proper burial," he said, and then, searching to find something to say, he added, "Why didn't you tell me about Nan, Mr. Brewer?"

"Tell you? Tell you what, Mr. Travis? That I saw this girl, young, vibrant, pretty?" He shook his head. "Ah, she was a sight. Her hair was like flax, and her eyes reminded me of a still, spring sky in early morning before the sun burns the color from it. And when she spoke to me, the gentleness in her rushed out; her heart was full of fine things, Mr. Travis. I don't think she ever thought about being barefoot and having only one dress to her name." He paused to drink his whiskey. Travis again found himself embarrassed by the combination of sincerity in this man and the absurdity of his fulsome sentiments. For once, the lieutenant could not think of a suitable response. Fortunately, Brewer started up again, murmuring half to himself, "How can I know what drew me back to see her? Was it the yearning for love and gentility in her, reaching out to fill the void within me? Or did I find love in this loveless land after all?" He shook his head again and took out a handkerchief and blew his nose. "I'll never know the truth now, will I, Mr. Travis? For the rest of my life I'll carry with me the golden image of her, and wonder if I loved, really loved her." He picked up the whiskey bottle and held it on his lap. "Would you mind leaving me alone, Mr. Travis?"

Relieved, Travis said gently, "Of course," and left quickly.

He went out to the barn; three soldiers were on top, hammers working to put part of the roof back in place. Corporal Ardmore had a detail repairing the corral, and Travis found many things to occupy him.

The Indians were trying to restore some order to their

village; the wind had all but leveled it, and it was late evening before anyone found time to light a mess fire so they could enjoy a hot meal. As soon as they had eaten, the troopers found places to sleep and curled up in their blankets. Travis got out his leather bound dispatch case and wrote his account of the twister and the damage he had observed. This would go through official channels and when Brewer put in for money to repair the agency, this account would substantiate his claim.

The lamp remained lit in Brewer's quarters, and the hour was growing late, which worried Jefferson Travis a little, for at such a time a man shouldn't be too long alone. Not a man like Brewer.

A glance at his watch told him that it was nearly eleven, and he wondered if Brewer would resent an intrusion. Perhaps the man was drunk and had passed out; if so, he needed someone to put him to bed. Or he might be cold sober, working on the riddle of his emotions, in which case he needed someone to talk to.

Travis was about to act on his decision when he heard a pistol go off inside the headquarters building. The sound was not loud, yet it brought Busik awake.

"What was that?"

"A pistol. Come on!" Travis said, and trotted across the muddy yard and bounded over the porch. The main office was dark, but a sliver of light appeared beneath the door to Brewer's quarters; Travis flung it open and stepped into the room, Busik right behind him.

The acrid odor of burnt black powder teased his nose, then he saw Brewer sprawled in his chair, a stain of blood spreading over his left breast.

"Gawd!" Busik said softly.

The pistol, a small .32 Smith & Wesson, lay on the floor beneath Brewer's dangling hand. The man was still alive; he rolled his eyes and looked at Travis and tried to smile, then his head dropped forward and rolled a little, tethered by the lax neck muscles.

"Funny place for a man to shoot himself," Busik said.

Travis looked at the sad figure of Brewer. "He pointed the gun where he thought his trouble lay, sergeant. Well, I guess he found the answer."

"How's that, sir?"

"He told me earlier that he didn't know whether he was attracted to Nan Pearl because he was lonely, or because he loved her. I guess he made up his mind and decided that he couldn't live without her."

"It's a hell of a price to pay to find out, ain't it, sir?"

He looked at Busik. "Did you ever know any payment out here to be small? Brewer killed himself for a lot of reasons, Busik, but maybe he died easier because at least he could tell himself it was on account of the girl and not because he was a pathetic misfit. In the morning I want a burial detail made up. I suppose I'll have to take charge here until they send someone else." He sighed and waved his hand. "Go back to your blankets, sergeant. I'll stay the night out."

He got a blanket from Brewer's bedroom and covered him, then sat down in one of the leather chairs and smoked a cigar. The lamp needed refilling and he attended to this, then took off his boots and spurs and elevated his feet to a small table.

His stay at the reservation would have to be extended some; the property and Indians could not be left unattended, even for a week. The moment official representatives left, the Indians would break into the storehouse and gut it of provisions. That would really be something to answer for to Major Deacon.

By morning, he had reached his decision and called

Busik into the office.

"Sergeant, on my desk at Spanish Spring there's a letter in triplicate, requesting Sergeant Arness' discharge to retirement status. It isn't effective as yet because Major Deacon hasn't signed it. I want you to take three men with you and bring Sergeant Arness here. But before you see him, tear up those three copies."

"Yes, sir," Busik said, a smile touching his lips. "You want me to tear up the other too, sir, the one making me and Ardmore—"

"This detail can stand two sergeants," Travis said. "Besides, Arness may object at coming and I wouldn't want a corporal hitting a sergeant."

"Oh, he's bound to object, sir. Maybe I'd better take four men."

"You can handle it," Travis assured him. "I don't care how you do it, sergeant. Tied hand and foot if necessary. But I'll expect you back in three days."

"Yes, sir." Then he laughed. "I can just see Ben now, sir, when I tell him. He doesn't like to be crossed, sir. Makes him contrary as hell."

"Busik, that man was born contrary. Now get on with it."

Ten minutes later, Busik and three troopers rode out and Travis set about the job of handling agency business. He had an inventory taken and signed by two witnesses, then talked to the four men who worked with Brewer. They told Travis what their routine was.

Burial was at one o'clock and the Indians gathered to watch. From a Bible found among Brewer's things, Travis read a brief service. Then, since Brewer was a government employee and because it would impress the Indians, Travis had a volley fired over the grave.

108

In the days that followed, he learned a great deal about the Indians; since there was a change in command, they assumed that he could be argued and wheedled out of extra provisions before he learned better.

Travis was young—there was no arguing that but he was a long way from being gullible; the Indians didn't get a thing from him that wasn't their just due. He sent six men in six directions to contact homesteaders who had suffered property loss from the twister; he spotted them for the troopers on Brewer's map to save time. The soldiers were to inform them that if they needed anything to tide them over, they could draw from the agency stores.

This was hardly a procedure endorsed by regulations, but Travis figured that in such a time of emergency, the regulations could go out the window and they could argue about it later. All he thought about were the women and children living on the prairie who might be hungry and homeless; he intended to do something about that.

Some semblance of order had been restored to the agency; the buildings were repaired and the corral fixed. Then, from across the flats, Busik and his detail approached with Ben Arness in tow, although Arness seemed to be accompanying them without fuss. However, he was not in uniform, Travis saw, as they rode into the yard. Arness wore a dark blue suit, a fawn-colored hat, and when he dismounted, the front of his coat parted to reveal a star pinned there.

He came toward Travis as though he meant to fight. "Damn it, you're going to explain this to me! What the hell's the idea going back on your word?" He thumped his chest. "I've got civic responsibilities now."

"The army needs you," Travis said calmly, "and until Major Deacon signs the papers, you're still army." He dismissed Busik and the others with a nod, and this disappointed them, for they wanted to hear how this would come out. "Come on inside," Travis said, and waved Arness in ahead of him. He poured a drink for him, then said. "How bad was the twister damage in Spanish Spring?"

"It leveled half the town," Arness said sourly. "Not many hurt though; they found cover in time. Where's Brewer?"

"Didn't Busik tell you?"

Arness laughed without humor. "Since he got those stripes, he's too important to talk."

"Brewer committed suicide," Travis said.

"Good God, why?"

Travis shrugged. "Does anyone ever really know why? This whole sorry mess was too much for him. If it hadn't been one thing, it would have been another. He left no message." He reached out and flipped open Arness' coat, exposing the badge. "You people are like sheep, sergeant. So Owen Gates docilely stepped down so you could step in. General Thomas C. Wrigley's flunky!" Then he shrugged. "Well, you're still a sergeant and I'm your commanding officer, like it or not. Since you sympathize with the homesteaders, I expect you know every one within a radius of seventy miles?"

"I do."

"Well, I saw what happened to two places that were in the twister's path, sergeant, and I suspect there's more. I've dispatched six men to pass the word that we'll distribute staples from the agency stores until they get going again. I want you to take charge of that detail,

110

sergeant. You'll stay here and attend to the reservation duties until a new man is sent down from Fort Dodge."

Ben Arness stared dumbfounded at Lieutenant Travis. "You're going to give away government supplies? After all the fuss you made over—" He shook his head. "I don't understand you at all. And I can see why the general doesn't trust you; he doesn't understand you either."

Travis leaned forward and looked into Arness' eyes. "Sergeant, I don't like you, and I'm not going to pretend that I do. For my money, you're a 'sometime' soldier, when it suits you, but there's twenty-seven years of service experience behind you and I'm counting on that being stronger than your petty dislikes. This is a government post. Run it like one. And by God, if you don't, I'll personally drag you before a court-martial board. Do you understand that?"

"I understand—sir."

Travis grinned. "There, you sound like your small-minded, bigoted self again, sergeant. Be consistent. I can understand you better, and if I have to, I can even tolerate you. That really grates, doesn't it? You like to think that you tolerate me. Be honest with yourself, Arness. It isn't too late." He turned to the door and paused there. "I'll be gone ten days to two weeks. When I come back, you can do as you damned please."

Lieutenant Travis moved north with his men before sunup, and in the early afternoon they skirted a fair-sized buffalo herd; it took them half a day of traveling before the tail end of it was out of sight.

The next day they saw a hunters' camp in the distance, and, covering acres, skinned hides were pegged out to be fleshed; the flies were a thick torment,

111

and the carcasses were beginning to stink. The skinners worked while the hunters, who were the aristocracy of this operation, lounged in the shade of the wagons, drinking whiskey, smoking, and telling lies. A few busied themselves with the task of reloading cartridges for the next day's shoot, or cleaned their long-barreled rifles.

As the cavalry approached, one man detached himself from the others and came forward as though he didn't want the army in his camp. He was a rangy, whiskered man, in his early thirties, and his eyes were as wary as an Indian's. He wore a brace of Colt cap-and-ball pistols on crossed belts, and a huge knife scabbard was sewn onto the leg of his leather breeches.

He nodded his greeting and went on chewing tobacco. Travis asked, "Have you seen any twister damage? Any homesteader's soddy in ruins?"

"Fella," the hunter said, "I stay clear of them places." He pointed to the northeast. "But I heard Luke Spears outfit came across somethin' interestin'. You might ask him."

"Where do I find Spears?"

"The last I heard he was skinnin' out near Ash Hollow. Eight, maybe nine miles from here."

Travis looked at the staked-out hides. "Looks like you did all right."

"Fair. Maybe seventy, eighty hides. The herds're just startin' to move now. Be better in another week or ten days." He looked sharply at Travis. "Hey, we ain't goin' to have no Injun trouble are we? I mean, with the army movin' around, I thought—"

"Everything is quiet on the reservation," Travis said. "And thank you for the information."

They rode off in the direction indicated, made a night

camp, and got an early start in the morning. They found the site where Spears had camped; the ground was littered with rotting carcasses and scavenger birds hawked away as they rode near, protesting this interruption with loud cries.

Travis found the tracks made by Spears' wagons and they continued to follow them into the twilight. In the distance, the faint wink of a fire guided them and an hour later they came to the fringe of Spears' camp.

They were a wary, wild bunch, these hunters; there were a half-dozen rifles on Travis and his men when they came into the camp, and only after they were identified were the weapons put away.

Spears was a giant; bearded, loud-talking. "Can't be too careful," he said. "Been some bloody killin's over buff'lo hides." He laughed. "You fellas find a hole when the twister hit? It shook every building in Dodge and blew half the tents down, although it didn't come within thirty miles of the place."

Travis stripped off his gauntlets and stuffed them in his belt. "We stopped at another hunters' camp." He jerked his thumb in the direction they had traveled. "We asked if they'd seen any homesteaders in need of help, and the leader seemed to think you'd met up with some."

Spears' eyes flashed with a sudden anger. "That was Gadding, I'll bet. That son-of-a-bitch never could say nothin' good about a man. What'd he want to tell lies about me for?"

Spears was blustering and defensive without any obvious cause. Inwardly, Travis heaved a sigh. This looked like more trouble. He decided not to waste time on tact.

"You don't mind if we look around your camp, do

113

you?" he asked.

"Hell, sure I mind!" Spears roared. "Do we have to be inspected or somethin'?"

The hunters had a huge fire going; it threw a wide circle of light, clear back to the wagons. Most of the men sprawled about watching the soldiers, while the skinners, who were not social equals, stayed farther back with the teamsters. Busik, who was standing near Travis' elbow, nudged him and pointed, singling Travis' attention on one hunter who lay half under a wagon; he appeared to be holding someone.

"Go take a look there, sergeant," Travis said. He watched Spears as he said it, and it seemed to be just like the Rinks all over again; Spears tried to draw his pistol and Travis beat him to it. He grabbed his wrist, pulled the giant's arm out straight, pivoted and slipped under it, then threw Spears over his shoulder to the ground. He hit with a dull thud and the hunters started to their feet, but carbines clicked in the silence and every man held his place.

Spears did not get up; he just lay there and looked at Travis as though he couldn't believe it had really happened. Travis said, "I don't want to turn this camp into a slaughter yard, so I'd suggest you all sit still until I see what's going on." He nodded to Busik. "Go have that look."

"As Busik skirted the fire, the man under the wagon yelped and a naked girl jumped up and ran for the grass away from the camp. Travis had only to snap his fingers and two troopers ran after her. To Busik he said, "Bring that man here!"

The hunter resisted, and Busik had to hit him several times before he got him to cooperate. There was a struggle away from the camp, then the two soldiers

114

came back, the reluctant girl between them. Out of consideration for her, they kept her away from the strong light of the fire, yet Travis could see that she was very young, fourteen or fifteen, not fully blossomed into womanhood.

One of the soldiers wrapped a blanket around her and she drew it tightly to her and huddled on the ground, crying, bent forward as though she suffered from intense cramps.

To Spears, Travis said, "Who is she?" Spears shrugged and remained silent. "All right," Travis said. "We'll do this properly. Busik, disarm this camp and if anyone gives you an argument, settle it any way you have to."

"Yes, sir."

It took a few minutes to gather up all the guns and knives, but the hunters offered no resistance; too many carbines were pointed at them and the troopers behind them all wore hard expressions.

"All right, Mr. Spears, I'll ask you again: who is she?" He turned and looked at a nearby trooper. "O'Donnell, if Mr. Spears does not answer, you may hit him on the head with the butt of your carbine until he does answer."

"Gladly, sir," he said grimly. He flipped it around and gripped the barrel, holding it like a baseball bat.

Spears held up his hands. "Oh, hell, she's some nester kid we found wandering on the prairie. The twister got the rest of her family, I guess. What difference does it make?"

"Who found her?" Travis asked flatly.

Spears hesitated, then nodded to the man Busik guarded. "He did." Then he made an appeal to Travis. "What the hell, lieutenant, she wasn't nothin' anyhow.

They don't care what happens to 'em; one bed's as good as another."

The truth nearly made Travis sick, but he forced it down, forced himself to be coldly analytical. "How many of you raped this girl?"

One of the hunters in the background laughed and said, "Suppose we all give her a dollar apiece, then it ain't rape. That all right?"

"With your permission, sir," O'Donnell said in a hard voice. He handed his carbine to another soldier, walked over to where the man lay, and kicked him flush in the face. A cavalryman's boots are heavy—graceless but sturdy—and O'Donnell made sure he put plenty of power into the blow. The man was flung back unconscious, and no one seemed to care. His face was a ruin; a lifetime disfiguration had taken place in an instant.

"Very good, O'Donnell," Travis said harshly. He looked at the hunters with a hatred born of outrage, and in his mind was the urge to punish the whole lot of them. Yet in spite of his anger, he knew that he must think clearly. Whatever his decision, he had to make it stick. He wasn't at all sure that violating a nester girl was a capital crime on the plains, or whether he was empowered to make charges; his position was somewhat undefined. But his shocked morality told him he must do something, arrest them, get them before a jury. The thought flashed through his mind that a jury in Dodge City would be comprised of buffalo hunters who would be unable to see the wrong of this at all, but it was a chance he had to take.

Travis spoke to Spears. "I want the names of the men who violated this child."

"Go to hell," Spears said, and was promptly knocked

116

flat with the rifle butt. O'Donnell was somewhat of an expert. He hit hard, but only a glancing blow; enough to hurt Spears, yet not knock him out. The hunter lay back, blood dripping from his scalp. He looked at Travis and said, "Mister, if I told, I'd never be able to hire another man. When the girl was brought into camp, I said there'd be trouble over her. But whether my men are right or wrong, I've got to stick by 'em."

Travis understood this reasoning, yet he could not retreat from his own position. This was a tense moment, where the fate of military authority hung in the balance of a very young man's judgment. His enraged instincts told him to hang the lot of them, yet he knew that he must take a detached, unemotional stand, the stand that any good officer would take.

"Busik," he said. "Throw some water on that man over there, the one who shot off his mouth. Get him on his feet."

Busik found a slop pail and drenched the man, bringing him around. He had to help him up, and then hold him there.

"Can you hear me?" Travis asked. The man nodded feebly. "Then believe what I say. I want the name of the first man who violated this child. If you don't give it to me, I'm going to hang you from a wagon tongue."

This was completely unexpected to the hunters, and they stared incredulously at Jefferson Travis. They had expected a roughing up, and perhaps a week in the Fort Dodge guardhouse, but not a hanging. And they knew that he might do it, because other young officers had taken the law into their own hands, like the young lieutenant who had hanged the Apaches and started that Indian trouble in the Arizona Territory. Maybe he'd been wrong, and maybe he'd realized it later, but the men he'd hanged were dead just the same.

"He did," the man said, pointing to the hunter flanked by soldier guards. "He brought her in and got to her first." Then he shouted at the guilty man. "What did you expect, you son-of-a-bitch? That I'd hang for you?"

A stillness came into the camp. Then with a rush the accused man tried to break away, but the soldiers swarmed him, mobbed him to the ground, then brought him erect, his arms twisted cruelly behind him.

Spears struggled to his feet and grabbed Travis by the arm, thinking that now this man would be hanged. "In the name of God, you'd hang him for that? What is she anyway? Another year and she'd have been in some nester's shack!"

Rudely Travis pushed him away. "I'm not going to hang him, Mr. Spears. I'll let a jury do that for me." He pointed to the man Busik held. "Bring him along. You come too, Spears."

"What for? You got what you came for."

"We're going to backtrack a little," Travis said. "Back to the place where he found the girl." He locked eyes with Spears. "It occurs to me that if a man doesn't have the sensitivity to see the shame here, the crime committed, it follows that a jury of Dodge City buffalo hunters might not see it either. I just want to make sure, Mr. Spears, that this girl's family was killed *by the twister.*"

9

SERGEANT BEN ARNESS TENDED HIS DUTY WELL, NOT because he felt any particular dedication, but because he knew that Jefferson Travis would tack his hide to the stable door if he didn't. Grudgingly, Arness had to admit that the young lieutenant was as tough as any brigade commander he had ever seen. For a young upstart who didn't know much, he was positive as hell about what he did know.

The Indians who had been the terror of the plains just a few years before were now almost wholly dependent on the reservation for supplies. With the hunters slaughtering off the buffalo, the Indians were too lazy or too proud to plant crops, and seemed content to beg flour, salt, and anything else they thought they could get.

Then the nesters started straggling in, those who had been hit hard by the twister, and Arness saw that they were given enough staples to carry them along until they could get up a new soddy and round up the few head of stock they owned. With all his tasks Arness kept busy enough to forget for a time that Travis had pulled a sneaky trick on him, and how much he hated him for it.

Trooper Daniels and two men returned one day, bearing a dying man on a travois. It was late in the evening and Arness had him, brought into the storeroom; there was no sense in having him bleed on the office floor.

"Found him crawling on his belly," Daniels said, biting off a chew of tobacco. "I sent two men to backtrack him. The twister got the rest of his family."

119

He looked at Arness. "However, he's been shot."

For a moment Arness failed to recognize the man; he was dirty and hollow-cheeked, and pain drew his face into harsh, unrecognizable lines. "Ain't that Swain, from over near Buffalo Basin?" He turned and got a lamp and lit it; the light was growing poorer every minute. "Get some water and clean him up a little. We'll have a look at that wound."

Swain was forty-some, old for his age, for he had given youth to the land, hard land. First, that ten acres of rock and stump in Arkansas, then that forty acres of Illinois bottom land that had been worked out before he got it, and now, six years on the prairie, with nothing to show for it except a twister-leveled soddy, a bullet aflame in his stomach, and a mind full of overpowering regrets.

There wasn't much Arness could do for the wound except clean it; Swain was a doomed man, but he was making a fight of it, holding off until the last possible moment, and Arness wondered why, when it would have been easier to just let go and die.

"I'd better put this all down on the report," Arness said. "That goddamned lieutenant will want to know the details." He went back to the office and Daniels followed him. "The twister got the rest, you say?"

"Yeah, the old lady and his sons. The soddy just collapsed and buried 'em."

"Didn't he have a girl? What about her?"

Daniels shook his head. "No girl around, sarge. And we dug too."

"Well, if the wind took her, she ought to have been around someplace," Arness said.

"I tell you we looked, circling for over a mile around the soddy. That's how we come across Swain, crawling

120

toward the reservation. Sarge, how come he's shot? You know, that ain't no .44 in him, not and make a hole like that. A buffalo rifle?"

Arness shook his head. "I wouldn't want to say." He sat down and began to write. "Kind of look after him. Make dying as easy as you can. If he wants a drink, just take what you need from Brewer's liquor cabinet."

"All right, sarge." He took a bottle and went out, and Arness never thought to tell him not to drink any of it himself. He finished writing up the details and then went to the storeroom. Swain lay like a frail ghost, alive only in his eyes.

Arness knelt beside him and said, "Can you hear me, Swain?"

The man nodded weakly.

"Do you know where you are, Swain? You're at the reservation. You got a bad one. No time to ride to Spanish Spring for the doc. Can you tell me who shot you?"

It required a supreme effort to speak, and then it came out as a whisper. "Hunter."

Arness knew the man didn't have the strength to say much, so he worked out a system whereby Swain could answer him without speaking. "Swain, I'll ask questions that you can answer by yes or no. You nod or shake your head. Do you understand?" He did, so Arness went on. "Did the hunter shoot you after the twister?"

Swain nodded.

"Were you in the soddy? No? Away then. Were you alone?" He watched the sideways movement of Swain's head. "Your boy with you? Your girl then. Yes, the girl was with you." He paused to think. "Well, you had to be under cover or the twister would have got you. In a buffalo wallow? Were you taking cover in a buffalo wallow?"

Swain nodded and Arness smiled, feeling that he was getting somewhere. "All right now, what about the girl? Is she dead? Alive!" A puzzled frown wrinkled his face. "Wait a minute now. The hunter was in the wallow when you got there? He was? More than one? How many? Three? Six? Ten? Ten hunters! Swain, did the hunters shoot you to take the girl?"

When Swain nodded, Arness stood up slowly. "All right, Swain, take it easy. We'll do what we can." He went out, looking for Trooper Daniels, and found him leaning against the far wall swigging from the bottle. Arness took it away from him and clouted him on the jaw, then ordered him to the storeroom.

He went back to the office and wrote some more in the report, detailing his questions and Swain's answers. It made sense, the hunters taking the girl. An unprotected woman was considered fair game to them; this was just a hard, brutal facet of living on the prairie, and Indian women, caught alone, would stuff themselves with dirt to cheat the hunters. Arness knew all these things, knew also that it didn't help to feel anger over it; there really wasn't anything he could do about it.

Just sit and write it all down on a piece of paper while a man lay dying in the storeroom.

The day was the hottest Travis had so far endured; they were moving toward the reservation now, the three buffalo hunters bound and tied to their horses, surrounded by troopers. They found the buffalo wallow where they had all hidden to protect themselves from the twister, but Busik found some additional sign, a spore of blood, and the tracks of army horses.

It was clear that all movement was toward the

122

reservation.

Luke Spears had stopped pleading, stopped arguing the night before; he knew now that nothing he could say would deter Travis. In Spears' mind it was injustice for him to be brought along, for his responsibility ended when the guilty man had been singled out. He was sure that by the time Travis got through fooling around, he'd find his hides and wagons gone, stolen by his own men in his absence.

At last they came in sight of the reservation; a brassy noon sun was overhead, layering the land with an intense heat and glare. When they rode into the yard, Ben Arness came out, saw the girl, and let his jaw drop open.

"Good God! I've got her old man in the storeroom with a bullet in him."

Across Lieutenant Travis' unshaven cheeks came a new brittleness. He whipped his head around and looked at Luke Spears. Then he said, "Separate these three men and keep them under close guard!" He pointed to the one who had taken the girl. His name was Clayman, originally bound for California, but he couldn't find a wagon train that would tolerate him, and he didn't have the courage to go it alone. "I want him brought to the storeroom. Hold him outside until I'm ready."

He lifted the girl down, taking care to keep the blanket around her to shield her nakedness. Then he carried her inside, to Brewer's room, and put her on the bed. Ben Arness was hovering by the door when Travis came out.

"She hasn't said one word since we recovered her," Travis said. "Oh, why couldn't they have a doctor here!" He slapped his hands together impatiently. The tension of his duty was beginning to show on him; his

123

face seemed even more thin and haggard, and his deep-set eyes more sunken. Small worries and larger ones kept pushing a wrinkled frown into his forehead, and the old optimism was gone from his voice, replaced now with a tired stubbornness, a determination to do the best he could with the inferior tools at hand.

"You look like you could stand some sleep, sir," Arness said.

"Later, later," Travis said irritably. "Is the girl's father still alive? Tell me about it." He listened to Arness relate the facts as he knew them while they walked toward the storeroom. Two haggard troopers guarded Clayman; the others, Spears, and the badly beaten man, were kept apart so they couldn't talk up a story between them.

"Bring him inside," Travis said, and opened the door. Swain rolled his eyes and stared at them as though he couldn't tell one from another, then he slowly raised his hand and pointed to the prisoner, his mouth working desperately.

"That's enough for me," Travis said harshly. "O'Donnell, this man remains bound and under strict guard; he is to speak to no one. Understand?"

"Yes, sir! I sure do." He gave the man a jolt with the rifle barrel. "Let's go, you son-of-a-bitch."

When the door closed, Travis took off his kepi and wiped his sweat-streaked face on the back of his sleeve. "If he dies, I've got a charge of murder to bring."

"In Dodge, sir?" Arness shook his head. "A jury of buffalo hunters would never convict him. It's the way the world is, sir. Buffalo hunters bring the money into Dodge, and even a merchant, if he was on the jury, would think of his cash drawer and not Swain shot in the belly." A trace of anger crept into his voice. "No one

124

would want the buffalo hunters to get down on them. And they're going to hate you, sir."

"Do you think I give a goddamn about that?" Travis snapped. He knelt by Swain and touched him lightly, bringing the man's eyes half open. "She's safe now, Swain."

He tried to smile, and he thanked Travis with his eyes. Then the two men stood there while Swain's breathing turned harsh and ragged; he took in a huge breath and let it out in a long sigh. He never took another.

Without thinking, Ben Arness slowly took off his hat and said softly, "He was grateful, sir, for telling him he didn't have to hang on no longer." Then angrily he wiped his knuckles across his nose and sniffed. "God damn it anyway, that's all they do, hang on, when there ain't nothin' to hang on for. And when one dies, another comes to hang on in his place." He jammed the hat back on his head. "I'll take care of the burial, sir."

"Yes, I'd appreciate that," Travis said, looking at Swain. "You know, sergeant, there'll come a time when all the Swains and the Pearls, who lived a lifetime being nothing, are going to be empire builders; that's what people will call them. Populating the prairie, as Wrigley said. Bringing schools and roads, hell! They brought blood and poured it on the ground, a man a mile, sergeant, a family an acre; that's what this land's going to cost, and there's no denying it!"

He wheeled and strode out into the smashing sunlight, motioning for Luke Spears to be brought to the office.

"Sit down," Travis snapped. He took his place behind the desk and eyed Spears coldly; there was not one shard of sympathy in Jefferson Travis. "Mr. Spears, I'm not going to mince words with you. Swain died, and Sergeant Arness tells me you were there when he was shot. Now I've got a charge of murder to bring against Clayman, and I'm going to enjoy watching him hang for it." He picked up a stub of a pencil and some paper and spun them around so that Spears could write. "I want you to put down everything that happened, just as it happened, and then you're going to sign it, before witnesses."

Spears licked his lips. "God, I can't do that! Why, when word got out, I'd be shot in the back inside of a month!"

Travis tapped his finger on the desk top. "Mr. Spears, you're done for anyway. If you don't write me a correct and complete account and sign it, I'm going to turn you loose on the prairie without a horse or a gun, and I'm going to make sure every Indian on the reservation knows about it. How long do you think you're going to last out there?"

"Why, that's plain murder!"

"It's more of a chance than Swain had, or that poor girl. Make up your mind, Mr. Spears. I'll give you thirty seconds." He took out his watch and laid it on the desk.

Spears didn't need thirty seconds; he was writing by the time fifteen had passed, Travis watched him labor over the paper, then he called in Arness and another soldier to witness the date and signature.

"Give Mr. Spears his horse and pistols and escort him a mile away from the reservation," Travis said.

This seemed to outrage Arness. "Are you turning him loose?" Then he shrugged and took Spears outside.

The beaten man was brought in; he was in considerable pain, for many of his teeth had been broken, and Travis suspected that his jaw was fractured too. He mumbled his story while Travis took it down, and it was signed with an X, and witnessed.

Then he was released and sent away from the reservation. Arness remained in Travis' office, and the young officer kept shuffling the two confessions. "You think I'm crazy, don't you, sergeant, letting two witnesses leave?" He smiled grimly. "A man can lie on the witness stand, sergeant, and he can be discredited by good cross-examination. But did you ever hear of a deposition being cross-examined or discredited?" He slapped the papers. "Here's my case, sergeant. Now have Brewer's ambulance hitched up. I want a detail of four men to escort me to Spanish Spring."

"What about the girl, sir?"

"I'm taking her along; she can't stay here. And even if she won't talk, sergeant, I want her on that witness stand to point her finger." The depth of his rage was apparent then, and Arness studied him carefully.

"Sir, every time I offer advice, you shut me up, but this time I wish you'd at least hear me out."

"All right. At least you're speaking to me again."

Arness grinned in spite of himself. "Well, what I've got to say is going to sound like I give a damn about you one way or another, and I don't. But I wish you'd think this over careful, sir."

"Meaning?"

"Well, the army around Fort Dodge is in sympathy with the buffalo hunters. Now if one of their patrols had run into this, most likely it'd have been written up in a report and let go at that. What I mean to say is, that if Clayman gets hung, a lot of people are liable to ask if this was the first time, or has it happened before. And the army at Dodge ain't going to like answering that, sir. Neither is Major Deacon." He scrubbed a hand across his weathered face. "Damn it, I don't like to sound as though I'm siding with Clayman—you know that ain't so—but I don't want to see a stink stirred up between the army and the buffalo hunters either."

"That happened when Clayman shot Swain," Travis said firmly. "I couldn't turn my back on this if I wanted to, sergeant. It's the way I am." He got up and turned toward Brewer's room. "Let's look in on the girl."

She was awake, lying still, staring at the ceiling, and when Travis stood by the bed, she moved only her eyes. She was pretty, in a big-boned, peasant way.

"How are you feeling?" Travis asked gently. "Can you understand me?"

She nodded, and he smiled to reassure her.

"We're going to take you to Spanish Spring, where you'll be safe. Wouldn't you like that?" When the girl did not answer, he looked at Arness. "Do you suppose there's something wrong with her? She doesn't say anything, just looks at you. I'm sure she understands."

Arness softly cleared his throat, then said, "Little girl, your father's dead."

"Why you clumsy—!"

Then Travis stopped, for the girl began to sob, with a grief made more terrible by its silence. He stared at her while her mouth worked frantically, trying to form words her voice box was incapable of producing. He could bear only a minute of this, then he wheeled and walked out of the room. Arness joined him a moment later and found Travis leaning against the wall, his face ashen.

"Mute," Travis said. "I understand now, sergeant; she was just a female animal to Clayman, just something to be thrown away." He waved his hand. "Go on, get Brewer's ambulance hitched up. I want to leave within

128

the hour."

Major Deacon was seven hours out of Fort Winthrop on the Spanish Spring road. He rode in an army ambulance, with the driver, and four troopers bringing up the rear. The heat and the dust bothered Deacon and he sat glumly on the high seat, a cold cigar clamped between his teeth, trying to ignore the many miles he had yet to go.

A dispatch case rested between his feet; in it were his personal papers and dispatches from Lieutenant Jefferson Travis. Major Deacon was suffering a twinge of conscience, for in assigning Travis to this detail he did so with the deliberate intent of using him and sacrificing him if necessary, for it was less tragic to lose an officer whose career had only commenced, than an officer whose career was already established.

Of course this was not the first hopeless assignment the army had suffered through; Ralph Deacon had lived through one or two when he had been younger, and expendable, himself. This was why his conscience troubled him, for in Jefferson Travis he now recognized value in spite of youth, and judgment, a sense of justice that was not misplaced by odds. The young man had honor and a capacity for greater things, if he could be spared.

Major Ralph Deacon was going to spare him, if he could.

It was bad to have to sacrifice a young, unproven officer whose worth had not yet been established. But it was criminal to sacrifice one whose worth was rapidly becoming apparent. In going to Spanish Spring, in supporting Travis, Major Deacon was placing his own future on the block, yet he disregarded the risks. Fort

Dodge was commanded by a general, and generals always protected themselves. And Fort Winthrop was an outpost, with only a tired major in command; he had no illusions about who would win in a test of political strength.

Still he had to try, because a damned young, inexperienced officer was trying, and this, in a way, was shaming Deacon to try with him.

They made a meal stop at the stage relay station, and quite coincidentally, the stage came through, which gave them an opportunity to catch up on the Spanish Spring gossip. Deacon ate alone, but the room was small enough for him to hear every word that was said, and in this way he learned of Swain's murder and Clayman's arrest.

Changing horses, Deacon and his detail moved on, at a faster pace now; he was in a hurry to get to Spanish Spring, for this was a development of tremendous importance and he could only speculate on the final results. The dead nester would be stoutly defended by politicians interested in clearing the buffalo hunters out and opening the land for farmers, and likely some Eastern newspapers would get hold of this and play it up. This would set the defenders of the hide hunters into action; they'd make a fight of it to protect their interests, which ran into several million dollars a year.

By George, he didn't want anyone turning this into another Dred Scott affair, and it could; a good many momentous things started out innocently enough.

Travis sat in his office in Spanish Spring and looked out the open door at the brassy sunlight. The sky was rinsed to the palest blue, and the country around had a purple cast, as though it stretched so frighteningly far that God tinted it so you could not see the full enormity of it.

A bath, a shave, and a change of clothes refreshed him; then he went out and down the street to Doctor Summers' house. Hope was in the kitchen humming to herself when Travis stepped into Summers' office. The doctor was grinding some white pills into a powder, and he went on with this while Travis sat down. When he had finished, he glanced at Travis and read correctly the embarrassed expression on the young man's face.

"Would you rather read a report of my examination, or have me tell it to you?" Summers asked.

Color came into Travis' cheeks. "Really, doctor, I know what goes on, you know. When I was fourteen, my father took me to a farm to watch a mare bred."

"I hardly consider that ample qualification," Summers said wryly. "But no matter. There's nothing wrong with her, no real harm done. Of course we ought to wait a few months to be positive of that." He poured the powder into paper sacks and folded them, then turned around to face Travis. "She's a husky girl, Mr. Travis. Perhaps we can find work for her someplace, housekeeping or something. Too bad this had to happen though. People will always remember it and point."

"Why do they do that? Why don't they point at a man because he broke his leg?"

"You answer that," Summers said, "and you've gone a long way toward solving the world's trouble." He slapped his thighs and stood up, reaching for his bag. "Got to peddle my pills. Hope's in the kitchen."

Travis went to the rear of the house while Summers slammed out the front door. Hope Randall was plucking a chicken; she wiped her hands on a towel and poured a cup of coffee for him. Then she sat down.

"You look older, Jeff."

131

"I'm a hundred years old," he declared. "And I wish I were ten again and running barefoot in a clover field with my dog." He laughed. "His name was Fleas and he was of mixed parentage, but he was a good dog. A farmer killed him with a pitchfork one day for scaring his horse, and no one ever did anything about it."

She regarded him steadily. "I could have guessed that last part, Jeff. But you'll break your heart, defending people who won't defend themselves."

"What would you have me do, Hope?"

"Just what you are doing," she said softly. "And one of these days I hope you'll find time to marry me."

10

IT WAS DUSK WHEN LIEUTENANT TRAVIS REACHED the archway to the barracks compound and saw the ambulance parked in front of his office. He stopped and stood there for a moment, trying to imagine where it had come from. Certainly it had brought a visitor of field grade; few below that rank rated an ambulance and a mounted escort.

His first guess was Major Griswald from Fort Dodge, and Travis walked on to the office with misgivings; he did not like Griswald, his opinions, or his manner. Two troopers whom Travis had never seen before stood on the porch. They came to attention as he stepped inside and saw that it wasn't Griswald at all.

Major Ralph Deacon was studying some papers. He raised his head as Travis saluted.

"At ease, Mr. Travis." He got up from behind the desk and waved Travis into the chair. "I hope you're not assuming that I've taken over your detail by occupying your chair." He shuffled his papers together and stuffed them into his dispatch case.

With a touch of nervousness, Jefferson Travis sat down and looked at Major Deacon. The lamplight struck the older man's face harshly, blocking it in defined shadows, giving his expression severity. Deacon opened his cigar case and bent forward to offer one to Travis. A match passed between them, then Deacon said, "Mr. Travis, can you smell trouble in the wind?"

"I'm learning how, sir."

"Mmmm, well, I could smell it all the way to Fort Winthrop." He crossed his skinny legs and rested his

133

hands on his knee. The cigar bobbed as he rolled it from one side of his mouth to the other. "You're very prompt with your reports, Mr. Travis. Very well written too. Very complete." He tapped his dispatch case. "I have a letter from Major Griswold requesting that you be relieved of your duties and returned to Fort Winthrop to be given a less exacting task. General Thomas C. Wrigley also wrote to me; he demands that you be withdrawn and a more experienced man replace you. Mr. Brewer, the Indian agent, wrote a letter to me complaining that you disrupted a beef issue and spread discontent among his charges. Mr. Travis, you seem to have a talent for antagonizing people."

"Yes, sir, if you want to look at it from their point of view."

Deacon's eyebrow raised. "Suppose you tell me your point of view then."

"May I speak freely, major?"

"It was an invitation," Deacon said. "Let's dispense with the protocol. We'll get more accomplished that way."

Jefferson Travis wiped a hand across his mouth and wondered where to begin. "Since I've assumed my duties, I've tried to pinpoint responsibility for the conditions that exist, and I've concluded that it's impossible, as such. My first impression of the homesteaders was that they were a thieving bunch. However, I now believe differently; they are more victims than perpetrators, major. General Wrigley, through some vague Indian Treaty stipulations and squatter's privilege, has taken charge of the decent land." He smiled. "I'm not suggesting that much of it is decent, but there *are* a few springs and water holes about that will support small-scale subsistence farming.

134

Wrigley claims control of this land and leases it to these people. Frankly, I seriously doubt the validity of his right to lease. But, be that as it may, he extracts what little money these people make, money they desperately need to live and grow on. In my opinion, he holds them in virtual slavery, much in the same manner as the New York landowners during the Dutch rule." He puffed on his cigar a moment. "The first contact I had with the cattlemen did not leave me with a favorable impression of them. They were arrogant and strong-willed, and I thought they were overly eager to take issue with the homesteaders. But this did not prove to be the case. Most of their grazing land is now Indian reservation, the homesteaders have been rustling them blind, and I now realize that had they been less tolerant, less peaceful, men would have been hanged before now. I came to terms with them, major; I found them quite reasonable." He paused and frowned a little. "As you know, Mr. Brewer is dead, and I hesitate to speak of his shortcomings now, but he was a man in a hopeless position, and, I believe, quite ill-fitted for the job. But I couldn't say what man would be fitted for *that* work; he would have to be a master diplomat, an excellent politician, a sharp horse trader, and something of a petty embezzler to come out on top."

Major Deacon laughed softly. "Mr. Travis, that is an astute observation. I must remember that. But go on."

"The buffalo hunters are a scurvy lot, major. Yet I can't condemn a man because he has a dirty neck. They are a product of the country, born of necessity. Without the buffalo they would not exist at all, so they can hardly be at fault for doing what is required of them. Buffalo robes are in vogue, and 'beaver' hats, so the buffalo have to be killed, and hide buyers in Dodge pour money into the town, and the army is there to protect the money." He shook his head. "It isn't my intention to lay the blame at anyone's door, major. I only wish to keep the multitude of forces here in harmony with one another. Without that, none of them can survive long." He fingered the ash off his cigar and sat with his elbows planted on the desk top, his hands cupped together. "I'd very much like to be thirty, major, with the experience to tell me what is right and wrong. But I'm not. I can only function within the scope of my own conscience, and stay as neutral as possible." He then went into lengthy detail, relating to Deacon the aftereffects of the twister, and the steps he had taken to relieve the hardships of it. "Of course I'll put this all down in a written report," he said. "At the moment, Sergeant Arness is in charge of the agency. In a week or ten days I expect someone will be sent out to take over. Which brings me to a most unpleasant matter, major." Quickly, in an unadorned fashion, he gave Major Deacon all the facts leading to the arrest of the buffalo hunter. While he talked, Deacon listened to the subtle changes in Travis' voice and realized how deeply disturbed the young man was over this affair.

"Are you going to press for a speedy local trial and a quick hanging?" Deacon asked.

"No, I've decided to make a public matter of it. I realize, sir, that such a decision may be unfavorable with the major, and of course you may change it."

"Mr. Travis, you'll be forcing the entire command at Fort Dodge to stand behind the buffalo hunters in the matter. They've always supported the hunters and the money behind them; they can't reverse their position now. Do you fully understand that the commanding general may feel as you do, yet, by prerogative, must publicly take the other side? Mr. Travis, for that your career may be forfeit."

"Yes, I understand that," Travis said. "I could try the man speedily and get him hanged and have it blow over with just a local smell to it." He spread his hands in an appeal. "Major, I could let that man go too, but if I did that, I'd be endorsing the molestation of every homesteader in this area, especially if he had a woman about. So you see, a quick hanging smacks of 'lynch justice,' and turning him loose is an acknowledgement by the U. S. Army that we have no justice at all." He sighed and chewed the end of his cigar. "Major, this is undoubtedly my first and last tour of duty, and I wouldn't like to leave anything behind that I'd be ashamed of."

Deacon studied him carefully. "You're willing to air this in a federal court in Dodge, Mr. Travis? The defense will wheel out the big guns; they'll rip you to pieces."

"Yes," he said.

"Justice against money! That's what will be on trial, Mr. Travis. The army policy." He snuffed out his cigar in a glass dish. "Dodge has needed a federal marshal for a year now, but no one wants to hire one. And the army has been nursemaid and protective father and whipping boy too long, but no one wants to change that either. If you win your case, Mr. Travis, some Washington politicians are going to have to overhaul their thinking and introduce some law out here. They'll have to give us more money, more men, and a sound policy. And I don't think they want to do that. They want the profit without the investment. The homesteaders are to shift for themselves, the hunters can do as they damn please, and the Indian has to stay where he's put as long as he's out of the way. But if you lose, Mr. Travis, it will signal in a new, prolonged period of lawlessness and bad politics, with every man shifting for himself toward his own ends. Do you think you have the right to gamble with the future of these people?"

"No, I don't," Travis said. "But I've got to take the right. Someone has to, major. I've got less to lose than perhaps the next man."

"You've got more to lose," Deacon said softly. "Well, I'd probably retire a major anyway, so that puts us in the same boat." He half rose from his chair and reached across the desk to offer his hand. "Now let's get together on our campaign strategy. I'm just the officer who can do a good job of prosecuting."

Lieutenant Travis had to return to the reservation; Sergeant Arness sent a trooper with word that the Indians were doing a lot of dancing and face-painting over the buffalo hunting. The kill was big this year and the Indians were scrounging around for powder and lead and talking war talk.

In going on to the reservation and leaving Major Deacon in town, Travis missed the transfer of the prisoner to Fort Dodge, six days' ride to the north. And he missed the communications the commanding officer of Dodge sent down to Major Deacon. The correspondence was essentially a threat with one end in mind, getting the charges against the hunter dropped.

The people of Spanish Spring were still busy repairing their roofs and fixing the twister damage, but the weekly paper managed to get published on time and the editor ran a well written account of the hunter's arrest. He editorialized about the crime, voicing a strong opinion, and copies of the paper went East on the stage when it came through. Ralph Deacon considered this inevitable; some reporter was bound to read about it and pick it up, because people always took an interest in what happened to the downtrodden.

Arriving at the reservation, Jefferson Travis learned that over forty braves had taken their horses and weapons and left the reservation, striking north into the buffalo hunter's territory. With this immediate crisis facing him, he deliberately ignored Arness' report that the agency stores were being rapidly depleted and that with no money coming from Washington for another six months the Indians would starve if something wasn't done. Leaving orders with Busik and Arness to ready the detail and be ready to leave with him at dawn, he slept the clock around.

The rest made him feel better. He arose before dawn, shaved, had something to eat, and was outside preparing to mount his horse before the sky in the east rinsed to a pale gray. He had to chance that the agency help would be able to manage alone. Travis couldn't spare Arness or any of his men to do the job, not when there was Indian trouble afoot.

Through a hot, dusty day they traveled in a sweeping circle, trying to pick up some sign of the Indians, and they camped out the night in a dry wash before pushing on. In the early morning they came across a buffalo hunters' camp and found three skinners digging graves.

Turning the detail over to Sergeant Arness, Travis went forward and spoke to the owner. "Indians?"

"God damn Indians," the man said, spitting tobacco juice. There was blood on his pants leg; he had suffered a slight wound, but paid it no mind. "They hit us late yesterday. We wasn't ready for nothin' like that." He squinted accusingly at Travis. "Thought you sojers was supposed to keep the Indians quiet. Can't you do your job?"

"How many in the raiding party?" Travis asked, side-stepping an argument.

"Oh, thirty-five, maybe a few more. You didn't answer me, mister."

"What the hell do you want to do, argue or tell me about the Indians so I can round them up?" Travis snapped. "How many casualties did you sustain?"

"How's that?"

"How many got shot?"

"Three dead," the hunter said. "Four wounded, but not bad. I got hit on my—"

"And the Indians?"

"I guess we killed five or six. They took 'em along though." He pointed to the east. "That way, if you intend followin' 'em."

"I intend to," Travis said, and went back to his horse. He swung about and struck off in the new direction, still on a cold trail, but it was better than nothing. Three dead hunters to five or six Indians was hardly profitable for the Indians. He supposed it was that way every year, the Indians going on a few punitive raids and getting their ranks thinned out, gaining absolutely nothing by it, for the government wouldn't blame the hunters. They'd blame the Indians for having a warlike nature.

Arness took the point and Busik came back to ride with Travis. He kept chewing tobacco and squinting and swinging his head from side to side to peer at the inscrutable distance. Finally he said, "Sir, what we going to do if we find the Indians?"

"Put them back on reservation."

Busik seemed saddened by this. "Sure is a shame, sir."

Travis looked at him. "What is?"

"Ah, you can't blame 'em for having blood in their eye, with the hunters killing off the buffalo and leaving the carcasses to rot. And it's a damned shame we've got to fight 'em to make 'em go back. It don't seem fair, somehow, for the Indians to lose at both ends."

"Just chalk it down as another inequity," Travis said.

That evening they came across a homesteader and his family. They were repairing their soddy, and the two oldest boys worked with their rifles close at hand. Everyone seemed relieved to see the army, and the men came forward as Travis dismounted his detail by the spring.

"Name's Otis," the man said, extending his hand. He wore a faded pair of overalls, but they were clean, and he had shaved that morning; so had his sons. He pointed to the three women near the soddy. "My wife and daughters. These are my sons, Mike and Adam."

"Howdy," they said, and shook hands. "You look mighty good to us right now, lieutenant."

"How's that?" Travis said. "You have an Indian scare?"

"We sure did," Otis declared. "Around noon, a passel came through, made up for war, I tell you. Paint all over 'em, and their ponies. We ain't drew a decent breath since."

"Say," Adam Otis said, "ain't you the one who caught that hunter after he killed Swain?"

"News gets around," Travis said. "Yes, he's in Fort Dodge by now, awaiting trial."

Some of the pleasure vanished from their eyes. "Fort Dodge, huh? Well, I reckon *they'll* turn him loose. Too bad, too. We could stand a little law on our side." He looked at Travis as though he was presenting an argument. "We're not dirt, lieutenant. We came out here with two wagons, tools, enough supplies for a year, and six hundred dollars." He shrugged as though he realized this was getting him nowhere. "If you're after those Indians, I'd ride about seven miles east of here. Deer Creek has some water in it, and there's timber there. They were heading in that general direction."

"We may push on through and try to locate their camp," Travis said. "They already raided a buffalo hunters' camp and killed three men."

"Good for them!" Mike Otis said.

Travis shook his head. "We've all got to try to get along," he said. "It's hard, I know, but the only way."

"Sure," Otis said, "but it's hard to care about people that don't give a damn for you."

That was, Travis thought, the whole thing in a nutshell. He turned to his horse and stepped into the saddle and led them in the direction of Deer Creek.

Shadows began to lengthen and the prairie turned dark, although the heat of the day, imprisoned in the ground, radiated from it like a dying fire in a sheet-iron stove. There was a cold-ration stop of forty minutes, and cinches were loosened and the horses fed and watered lightly.

He kept thinking ahead, wondering if the Indians were camped at Deer Creek. It seemed logical that they would be, for they needed rest as well as the cavalry. But he wasn't sure of what he would do when he found them. Talking to them was out of the question. They had been lied to so many times that they refused to believe any white man. Fighting them seemed almost criminal. There were too many things in their lives to fight without adding the U. S. Army.

Yet he had to get them back, for their own sakes, and

142

this was an ironic paradox, for no matter what he said, they would believe he wanted them on the reservation for the protection of the hunters.

He had a chance to talk to Arness when he walked over to where he sat alone. "Major Deacon is in Spanish Spring," he said. "When we get back you can take your complaints to him. I give you my permission."

Arness raised his head and looked at Travis, then said, "To hell with it."

"You quitting, sergeant?" Travis squatted beside him. "I'm glad to hear it, because you can't beat me. I'd always have the rank and you know it. It's too bad you choke on it; we might accomplish a lot together, if you'd accept it." He took out two cigars and offered one to Arness, and when the sergeant shook his head Travis jammed it between his lips, a little out of patience. "Here. Stop being such a stubborn jackass." He raked a match alight on the seat of his pants and held it cupped near Arness' face. Then Arness laughed softly and drew his cigar alight.

"The last time we smoked a cigar, lieutenant, was because I wanted to see you cough a little. Now I guess it's my turn to cough." He took the cigar from his mouth and made some hacking sounds, then laughed again.

"Arness, did you ever try being honest with yourself about the army?"

"What do you mean?"

"Did you ever try to accept the truth for what it was? That you'd given a lot of years and felt that you hadn't got fair return for it?" Arness looked at him and Travis knew that he had hit on a truth. "Ben, what is it you want most from life? Give me an answer."

"A home and wife and some kids," Arness said. "I can't remember what it's like to sit under my own roof,

143

lieutenant. For twenty-seven years I've seen young officers come in the army and get married and raise their families, but it's not for an enlisted man, sir."

"Some do it."

"A wife of mine wouldn't live on Suds Row." He drew deeply on his cigar. "Look at me now, near the end of it, and nothing to show for it but nine hundred dollars in the St. Louis bank." He shrugged and stared at the ground. "Grace Beaumont is the only woman I ever asked to marry me. I felt I could, not having much more time to go. Still, it's not that easy, always being army, knowing you're no good for anything on the outside, and knowing you'll have to be out someday."

"So it suited you to have me 'push' you out, is that it? That way, if it didn't work, you could always blame me and not yourself." Travis shook his head. "Don't do that to me, Arness. I don't want any part of it." He got up and looked down at Arness. "It takes a man to stand on his own two feet. Maybe you like the army because there's always an officer around to give you an order, and when it goes sour, you can say it was his fault and not yours. The army isn't something to lean on, Arness. You've got a little part of it to hold up. And I wish to hell you'd try and do that."

"Where'd you hear that, at the Academy?"

"As a matter of fact, I did. It's still true." He started away, then turned back. "When we get to Spanish Spring, ask Major Deacon to make out your retirement papers. Or else get a transfer out of my detail."

"What for? I thought we were beginning to understand each other."

"Just understanding something doesn't make it right," Travis said, and walked away. Busik was stretched out on the ground, a hand over his face; he stirred when

144

Travis came up.

"Get the men mounted, sergeant. Let's get on with our Indian hunting."

A few minutes later they were again moving toward Deer Creek, and in an hour they came upon it, a trickle of water in an irregular slash across the flat face of the prairie. The night was dark, with only a splinter of moon to help them, and Travis led his men slowly and quietly along the creek for better than a mile and a half.

Then he stopped and let them bunch up. Ahead was a grove of trees, and he thought he saw a camp there, the flicker of a small fire. Leaving Arness with the detail, he and Busik went forward afoot for a closer look.

It was the Indian camp. The horse herd was being guarded on the other side, two braves moving around them constantly. The fire was built low in the creek bed, and in that way shielded from the view of anyone approaching from the north or south. And even if a man traveled along the twisted course of the creek, he might stumble on the camp before he saw it.

There was no accurate way to count the remaining Indians, but Travis thought that thirty-five might be a fair estimate. He motioned for Busik to move back, and followed him, and when he rejoined his detail, he took off his kepi and wiped his forehead.

"You want a flanking maneuver, sir?" Arness asked. "We can catch them in a cross fire."

"I don't want anything of the sort," Travis said testily. He wondered whether or not he should berate Arness for presuming to advise him in front of the men, then decided not to. "We'll make a quiet camp here," Travis said. "Then, before dawn, we'll make a raid on the Indian ponies. It occurs to me that they can't make much war afoot." He looked intently at Arness. "And

145

the first man who downs an Indian when we go in can figure that he's in more trouble than he ever knew existed. I want those Indians back on reservation all right, but unharmed. They've already had enough done to them."

11

IN THE CREEK BED, TRAVIS' MEN WAITED SILENTLY, the horses held well back. Six hundred yards separated them from the Indian camp, and there was no sign of movement there either. Some of the troopers caught up on their sleep; they were a calm lot, undisturbed over the prospect of trouble.

Travis stretched out on his back, his heels near the trickle of water, but he could not sleep. There were only two ways to disarm the Indians: take their guns away from them, or their horses. Fewer would be killed if he took their horses. Afoot, the Indians couldn't do much except return to the reservation. The scare would be over and the damned hide hunters could go on killing the buffalo until they were all gone. Then they could move on to something else, for it seemed to be their lot to destroy. Travis had read much about the mountain men, how they raped a country of her furs in a few years, and with their greed destroyed their own way of life. The buffalo hunters just might do the same thing, but the damage would be done by then. The Indian would have nothing to hunt, no way to live, and in time they too would vanish, killed off by "progress," or shoved out of sight on some reservation and forgotten.

About three o'clock he woke Busik and quietly the men mounted up and left the creek bed, easing in toward the Indian camp. Travis made certain he was on the same side as the pony herd; he didn't want to have to charge across that creek bed full tilt, and in the darkness to boot.

The Indians' ponies were bunched up, just clear of

the stunted timber, and guarded by two mounted warriors who rode sleepily about. Travis moved close enough so that he could just make them out, then he waved his hand and the men moved into a line abreast to wait for his signal. He gave it with a jab of spurs and they thundered toward the pony herd, yelling and whooping, and the two guards wheeled to meet them. The Indian camp came alive with a rush, but it was too late. Travis and his men were into the herd, driving them out. Guns popped as the two guards fired at the soldiers, but there were no answering shots. Some of the Indians in the camp loosed a volley at the vanishing horses, then Travis and his men were in the clear, pushing the herd onto the flats, beyond hope of the Indians' recovering them.

Busik and the men gathered the ponies and held them, and Travis signaled for Arness to side him. When he drew up, Travis said, "There are still two mounted men in that camp, Ben. And two Indians on horseback constitute a danger. Let's go back."

"You're crazy, sir."

"I don't think they'll expect us," Travis said. "I want those two ponies, Ben. The Indians are going to walk back to the reservation so they won't forget this." He twisted in the saddle for a look around. "Two mounted men *could* try to take the horses back. Now let's go; I'm picking you to volunteer."

"All right, since you put it that way."

They made another approach to the Indian camp. It was in an uproar, braves milling about, shouting, blaming everyone else for the surprise attack. The fire was being built up, and the two mounted guards rode about, shouting at those on foot. They were so busy arguing that Arness and Travis made their approach unnoticed. They were almost into the camp before the Indians spotted them.

One of the mounted braves wheeled his horse and whooped, leveling his rifle to fire at Travis as he came at him. Bending low, Travis made a small target of himself and the bullet missed him somehow. Then they came together and Travis caught the brave around the throat and dragged him backward off the horse. Arness and the other Indian were clubbing at each other with carbines. A gun went off and Arness grunted, then fell, dragging the brave with him. There was the sound of a bone snapping when they hit the ground, but Travis was too busy to pay much attention. He dragged the brave he had unhorsed into the camp and dumped him across the fire. With a shriek the Indian bounded up and went thrashing off into the brush, trying to put out the blaze in his breeches.

Travis was in the middle of the Indians, surrounded completely, and a rush of fear filled his chest, but he beat it down and dismounted as casually as he could. The Indians started to crowd about him, their half-naked bodies vivid with paint, their bronze faces cold and angry. He rammed his way through them and knelt by Ben Arness, who lay on the ground, clutching his stomach. Blood stained his fingers, but he managed a weak smile.

One of the Indians grabbed Travis by the shoulder as though to pull him away, and he was stopped by a shout. Travis looked around as a tall, well-proportioned brave stepped toward him. He wore broad white streaks across his nose and cheekbones, and he carried a Henry repeating rifle, the brass receiver dull and tarnished. A hoary ring of corrosion crowned the muzzle, for Indians never understood the necessity of cleaning their weapons.

"The soldier dies," the Indian said, speaking to the brave who had bothered Travis. "Leave this moment to him." He pointed to the Indian Arness had dragged from the horse. His neck was twisted at a grotesque angle, broken in the fall. "We have our own dead."

"Ben," Travis said, "how bad is it?"

"Hotter than—any whiskey I—ever drank," Arness said. He looked past Travis, at the Indians circling them. "Got yourself in—a tight one—this time, sir."

"Never mind that," Travis said. "We'll get you a doctor—"

"Too far," Arness said softly.

"You can hang on," Travis said. "Swain hung on. Are you still a damned quitter, Ben? Is that the way it's going to end? You not wanting to play it if you can't make the rules? Go ahead and die then. Who the hell's going to miss you anyway?"

He stood up and turned his back on Arness. "Who is the leader here?"

"I lead," an Indian said.

"Don't I know you? Yes, you're the one who talked so much at the reservation. Well, I thought then that you were a troublemaker. I guess I was right." He waved his hand to include them all. "Go on back to the reservation. The fighting is over."

There was no change in the Indian's expression. He still kept his rife pointed at Travis' stomach. "The soldier leader has a strong heart. Death is all around you, yet you speak of your terms. We do not go back, soldier leader. Many battles are to be fought before we die." A sound came to him then, so subtle that Travis did not hear it, but all the Indians looked around them.

Then Travis saw what had alarmed them. Busik and

ten men circled them, carbines ready. They had come in afoot, very quietly. And they waited for Travis to speak, to give the order for them to fire.

"*You* may die now," Travis said, "if you choose. There will be no more war with the buffalo hunters. You'll go back to the reservation afoot, for we have your ponies."

He didn't realize what an insult this was, for to return afoot would disgrace them in the eyes of the others. An Indian scorned another who lost his horse.

The rifle still pointed at Travis' stomach, and to quell his nervousness, he reached out and plucked it quickly from the leader's hands. A wail went up among them. Their defeat was certain now, and their future inevitable. This was just another degradation, and Travis supposed that the day would come when they would surrender on sight of a white man.

"Busik, rig a travois for Arness, he's been gut shot." He pushed the Indians aside and bruskly gave orders. "Have the horses driven to the reservation and corralled there. They'll be returned to their owners when each one steps up and surrenders his rifle and ammunition. The rest of you form a column of twos and we'll follow the Indians back, at a respectable distance."

"Herding them, sir," Busik said, "is going to be hard on their pride."

"It will hurt less than a bullet," Travis said, and walked to his horse and stepped into the saddle. He observed the activity from this advantageous position, for he thought that it might have some effect on the Indians, the conqueror sitting above them, watching them. A travois was made and Arness transferred to it with some groaning. One of the troopers kicked out the fire and the Indians were marched off. They still carried

151

their rifles, but Travis expected no more trouble from them. He had destroyed their confidence when he disarmed their leader, and the effect of this would take a while to wear off.

At dawn they were moving across the prairie, the Indians in a straggling knot a quarter of a mile ahead of the cavalry. Arness bobbed along on the travois, making a rough trip of it, but he endured his pain as silently as possible. When they came to a point that Travis reckoned as due north of Spanish Spring, he called Corporal Ardmore aside and instructed him to kill his horse riding for Doctor Summers. They would wait at the reservation.

That afternoon they passed near a homesteader, and he came out with his brood to watch the parade of Indians pass by, and when the cavalry passed, they all cheered and clapped their hands. Travis wished he could stop them, for it was bad enough to humiliate the Indians without rubbing salt into bleeding wounds.

He planned to march straight through to the reservation, with only a few rest stops, for dismounted men were very vulnerable on the prairie. They saw some skinners at work, and, to the north, they could hear the near-constant boom of heavy caliber rifles as hunters went on with the slaughter. Toward evening a good-sized herd thundered southward, passing them over a mile away. The dust hung in the air for an hour after they had gone by, and later, just before dark, a knot of horsemen rode down on them, hunters looking for stragglers and wounded from the herd.

When they saw the Indians afoot, they forgot their intent and changed course, making for them.

"Forward," Travis shouted, and brought his detail to the gallop. He planned to intercept the hunters' path, placing himself between them and the Indians, and his reckoning was correct, for he arrived just as the hunters drew up.

A huge bearded man was their leader. He pointed past Travis to the Indians and said, "How come you ain't killed 'em? Ain't that your job?"

"I know my job," Travis said. "Don't interfere with it."

The hunter looked at the eight armed men behind him, and at the dusty troopers, then laughed. "Well, sonny, you just ride on and we'll do it for you. Pete! Hank! Skirt that flank and put a couple of shots in 'em for the hell of it."

"The first man who lifts a weapon will be killed," Travis said. "At the ready!"

Spencers were flipped up and hammers came back. A surprised look came into the hunters' eyes, as though they had bitten into a nice piece of cake and found it full of walnut hulls. The leader, who wore a bone-handled pistol at his hip, put both hands on the pommel and looked at Travis.

"Sonny, you don't really mean that, do you?" His eyes hardened as he said, "Pete! Hank! You heard what I said?"

"You do it," one of them answered. "You're the boss, Swilling."

"Yeah, I am at that," Swilling said flatly. "Say, ain't you the bastard that shook up Luke Spears' outfit?" He grinned. "Well now, this is more interestin' than the Indians, ain't it, men?" He took a hand off the pommel and put it on his thigh, near his holster. The flap was unfastened, hanging loose over the butt of his gun, and Travis considered his own weapon, secured against his hip. He was at a bad disadvantage. "We ran across

153

Spears on his way to Dodge, sonny. Gave him and the other fella two horses. Spears lost his outfit, and he's offering three hundred dollars in cash to the man who kills you."

"Do you need three hundred dollars?" Travis asked, sparring for time. He watched Swilling's hand, and when it moved, he cast himself off the horse and hit the ground rolling, tugging at his pistol holster.

Swilling's first bullet spewed dirt over Travis' shirt sleeve, and the second plucked the kepi off his head and sailed it into the grass. Swilling never fired a third time, because Travis came to one knee, sighted his .44 Smith & Wesson, and shot Swilling dead center in the breastbone.

The man fell off his horse like a half-filled barley bag, and the horse shied when Swilling rolled against his legs. The rest of the hunters remained very still, staring at a row of .57 caliber Spencer carbines. As Travis got up and retrieved his kepi, he noticed that the bullet had rent the hard round top of it, and he tried not to think about the troopers and the way they had held their fire; perfect discipline. No soldier worth two bits would act without an officer's command.

With amazing calm—at least on the exterior—he broke open his .44 and inserted a fresh shell, then holstered the weapon.

"Does three hundred dollars seem inviting to anyone else? No? Then turn those horses around and get the hell out of here!"

"You won't be so lucky when you meet Spears," one man said, then they wheeled their horses and went back the way they had come.

Travis' hand trembled when he reached for the reins, and Busik saw it. Travis felt shame because it showed.

154

Then Busik laughed and said, "Sir, that wasn't bad pistol marksmanship."

"Thank you, sergeant." Travis was amazed at the effect of Busik's brief words. His nervousness vanished and complete control returned. He looked at Swilling a moment, then said, "God forgive me, I don't feel like burying him. But break out the shovels anyway, sergeant."

"Yes, sir."

While they were burying the buffalo hunter, Travis rode over to where the Indians hunkered down in the grass. He did not dismount, and the leader looked at him, an expression of puzzlement in his eyes.

"Does the soldier leader kill his own people?"

"When it is necessary."

"The soldier is a friend to the buffalo killers. It is so. Is there now war between the soldier and the buffalo killers?" He asked this hopefully.

"No," Travis said, and returned to see how the burial detail was coming along. Busik wasn't putting the man down very deep. They were getting ready to shovel in the dirt when Travis turned to Ben Arness on the travois and stepped from the saddle.

Arness' face was gray, and pain etched deep lines in it. He looked at Travis and tried to smile. "Thanks for—sending for Doc, sir."

"I only wanted it on the record that I tried," Travis said, trying to sound casual.

"You going to—miss me when I'm—gone?"

"Wait until you go," Travis said. "Maybe you'll just bleed some of the contrariness out of you. That's what they used to do in the old days."

"Wish I had a—drink."

"With a hole in your stomach it'd leak right out,"

155

Travis said. "Come on, Ben, be tough. For once in your life, live up to your reputation."

Busik came up. "Finished, sir."

"Then let's get going."

In the very last of the daylight they moved on toward the reservation headquarters.

Arness was put in a room and made as comfortable as possible. In Brewer's medicine chest, Travis found a hypodermic needle and some morphine, and from a leather-bound instruction book he found the proper dosage and method of administering it. This gave Arness relief from the pain and he sank into a deep, undisturbed sleep.

With the pony herd safely guarded in the corral, Travis set about his task in the morning to trade the horses for weapons. Word was passed about the village, and the response was better than he had figured on. Nearly sixteen braves came forward and surrendered their guns and took their horses back. For Travis this provided an insight into the Indian way of thinking. Their war had gone badly and since they had suffered defeat, they believed their gods frowned on the enterprise and were willing to abandon it.

Still there were some hardheads who would not give in, and he knew they had to in order to completely squash any notion they might have of breaking out again. So, taking Busik with him, he went into the village. He thought it best to go without more men behind him, to carry further the idea in the Indians' minds that the soldiers were superior.

Travis pushed his way into the first lodge and turned it upside down looking for guns, and when the Indians offered resistance, he knocked one down and kicked

156

another. He knew that this was a bold move, but they seemed to respect boldness, and often took no action just to see what was going to happen next. He found four rifles and some corroded ammunition, and then refused to part with any of the ponies when the braves wanted them back. All guns, he told them, that he had to get himself, were not worth a pony.

He gave them an hour to think this over, and by two o'clock his corral was empty and all the rifles and shells were locked in the storeroom.

This was, he hoped, the end of the Indian trouble for a while. He didn't think it would ever end permanently.

Quite late the next day, Major Deacon arrived in the ambulance, drawn by two lathered horses, with his four-man escort. Doctor Summers was with him and he rushed inside to have a look at Ben Arness, who was still stubbornly clinging to life.

Ralph Deacon sat down in the office and accepted one of Travis' cigars. Dust powdered the major's clothing and he had sweated through the back of his shirt. After he had blown a wreath of smoke to the ceiling beams, he said, "That damned General Wrigley is a pain in the butt, isn't he?"

"Yes, sir, a genuine pain."

Deacon shook his head. "Five years ago he was just a defeated Rebel. But the war's over and the Union generals are writing their memoirs and the Wrigleys now become proud, gallant foes, all remembered kindly. Naturally they take advantage of it and try to wheedle favors."

"What's the general been doing, sir?"

"Camping on my doorstep, that's what he's been doing. Good God, Mr. Travis, since you arrested that hunter, Wrigley thinks the army has entered into the

157

partnership of marriage with him. He's been telling me how to conduct the prosecution until I'm sick of it. He's even volunteered to go to Dodge and testify. That's why I came along with Summers. The reservation will be a relief."

"Any word from Fort Dodge about the trial date?"

"In ten days," Deacon said, his thin face full of concern. "I think the commanding general wants to get this over with before newspapermen get out here from the East. There are some advantages to this geographical location. The Indian scare didn't turn out to be much, did it?"

"No, sir, they really weren't in a position to make war against the hunters."

"But they always try. How many dead Indians am I going to have to explain away to the Department of Interior, Mr. Travis?"

"Well, none, sir. We stole their horses and marched them back to the reservation. Then I traded the horses for the guns."

Slowly Deacon removed the cigar from his mouth and stared at Jefferson Travis. "Do you mean to tell me Arness was the only man who was shot?"

"No, sir. I killed a buffalo hunter. There was a group of them bent on shooting a few Indians. However, the argument was personal. Spears has offered three hundred dollars to the hunter who kills me. This fellow, Swilling, was eager to collect it. In the exchange of shots, he was killed."

"Is that how you got that crease in the top of your kepi?"

Travis laughed and took it off. "Yes, sir. I thought I'd wear it as a reminder of how close a man can come to getting killed and still be alive." His expression grew sober. "Major, I haven't gotten us into any more trouble, have I? I mean, they're not going to make anything out of this Swilling affair, are they?"

Major Deacon shrugged his shoulders. "I don't know. Their version of it isn't going to agree with yours, I can tell you that." He got up and walked around the room, trailing cigar smoke. "This evening, I'd like to go over our case with you, Mr. Travis. You're familiar with court-martial procedure?"

"Yes, sir."

"Well, I imagine it'll be similar, only with a federal judge presiding. The army will want to keep as much control over this as possible. That's why it'll be held on the post, to keep newspapermen out. The prosecution will present its case first, then the defense will get a crack at us. Naturally we can recall witnesses for cross-examination." He came back and sat down. He seemed nervous, unable to be still. "Having practically memorized the two depositions you took, I've come to the conclusion that we're going to be outfoxed there."

"How's that, sir?"

"Well, if we introduce them, the defense will place Spears and the other man on the stand and dispute the depositions. Whether we like it or not, I think our safest course will be to accept Spears as a hostile witness and keep waving the deposition under his nose if his story happens to be different. But we'll talk about that later."

The connecting door opened and Doctor Summers entered the room. He tossed a .44 Henry rifle bullet on the table and then tamped tobacco into his pipe. "If that had been one of those new .44-40 '73 Winchesters, he'd be dead. It didn't do too much damage. I sewed up two minor holes in the large intestine, but the bullet didn't penetrate too deep."

159

"Is Ben going to make it?" Travis asked.

Summers shrugged. "Fifty-fifty. Depends on what complications he has, if any." He shook his head. "It's tough to say when you can't get the bullet out right away. A couple days should tell." He looked from one to the other. "Don't hold the wake yet."

"Hardly," Deacon said.

"Would you care for a drink?" Travis asked. "Brewer left some pretty good whiskey behind."

"Fine," Summers said, and sat down. He crossed his legs and sucked on his pipe, adding a strong flavor of shag tobacco to their cigars. "Hope sends you a kiss," he said, chuckling. "You want me to give it to you?" His amusement increased when Jefferson Travis' neck got red.

"There," the young lieutenant told him, "drink your whiskey."

Summers tossed it off, then wiped his eyes. "You say that's pretty good? It's a cross between formaldehyde and rubbing alcohol." Then he handed the glass back to Travis. "Fill it up again. And my blessing to Mr. Brewer, wherever he may be. There is, I believe, a very slight demarcation between some men's heaven and hell."

Ralph Deacon looked at him curiously. "Where's all the compassion for human suffering?"

"Buried in an ocean of tears," Summers said. He leaned back in his chair and smiled. "Gentlemen, before I die, I want to be called out in the middle of a stormy night, to drive eighteen miles through the mud, and when I get there I want to find a man who is healthy as hell, and just wanted to tell me so. What a refreshing change!" He looked at Jefferson Travis. "Say, you *are* going to marry my niece, aren't you? I'll bring your first

160

four children into the world for nothing. You can't ask for a better bargain than that." He held up his empty glass again. "Just a little more, and don't worry about me. I turn morose when I've had too much to drink."

12

WITH A BEEF RATION TAKING PLACE ON THURSDAY,
Janeway and five of his men drove a herd of cattle onto
the reservation early Wednesday morning, and that
afternoon Otis appeared with three gaunt animals. Later,
five more homesteaders showed up, one of them driving
a solitary steer.

To the penny, Travis knew how much cash was in the
agency safe, and he knew there wasn't enough to buy all
the cattle; not and pay cash for them. Busik was in
charge of the holding pens and the weighing in, and
Travis and Major Deacon observed the proceedings. In
deference to Deacon's rank, Travis offered to turn the
issue over to him, but Deacon declined, saying he would
rather watch.

Before the weighing began, Travis gathered Janeway
and the others around the scale and had it checked out
against the test weights to assure them that the agency
was dealing honestly. Travis allowed the homesteaders
to weigh in their beef first, and Busik kept a record of it.
The cattle were hardly in prime condition, and Travis
understood that they were being sold to get a little
"building" money to repair various bits of damage done
by the twister.

Janeway's cattle weighed in at an average of fifty
pounds more than any of the others, and Travis
questioned Busik about this. He didn't think that
Janeway's graze was that much better.

"Don't those bellies look a little round to you,
sergeant?"

"Yes, sir." Janeway was standing right beside Busik,

and the sergeant looked at him, then at Travis; he seemed reluctant to say any more.

"Well, sergeant, do you have an opinion?"

Otis and some of the others came over to lean on the pen rail; they could hear everything that was being said. Busik scratched the back of his neck. "Well, I wouldn't want to accuse anyone, sir, but I'd say it was possible they stopped at that seep about four miles from here and drank their fill of water."

"At six pounds to the gallon," Travis said, "that would add up." He turned to Janeway and found the man's face dark with resentment. "Well, Mr. Janeway?"

"Why, that's a hell of a thing to accuse a man of!"

"You couldn't prove it, sir," Busik said hastily.

"I suppose not," Travis said. "But I could confirm a suspicion, couldn't I? Sergeant, have Janeway's cattle weighed in, then held overnight. We'll weigh them again in the morning and see if they're any lighter." He tapped Busik's tally sheet. "Pay off Otis and the others on the weight."

"Yes, sir."

"Now, just a goddamned minute!" Janeway fumed. "You chivvied me into lowering the price of my steers, then you've got the gall to accuse me of watering in to make more weight." He shook his fist under Travis' nose. "Someone ought to give you a good thrashing."

"Mr. Janeway, if I'm wrong, I'll be paying you full weight, won't I?"

"It's the principle of the thing, that's all! You going to pay me now or in the morning?"

"In the morning, after they're weighed again," Travis said.

Janeway turned to Major Deacon, who sat on the top rail, smoking his cigar and chasing flies away from his

163

face. "Are you going to allow that, major?"

"What he proposes is fair," Deacon said dryly. "He tested the scales to show he was giving honest measure. It wouldn't hurt you to go along."

Janeway kicked dust and took off his hat and flogged it against his leg. "All right, I stopped at the seep and they drank a little. Hell, they were thirsty!" He looked at Deacon and his unreadable expression, then at Travis, who just seemed to be waiting. Finally Janeway snapped, "Take thirty pounds apiece off of 'em if you feel like it!"

"Mark that down, sergeant," Travis said. He spoke to the others. "Sergeant Busik will pay you off. Mr. Janeway, would you mind stepping into the office for a minute?"

Travis turned and walked across the yard, Janeway following him, and then Deacon said, "I think I'll go listen to this," and jumped down off the top rail.

Inside, Travis poured a drink for Janeway, then another for Major Deacon when he came in. He sat down behind his desk and folded his hands. "I'm going to pay you in cash for twenty-one steers, and in army script for the other nine," he said.

Janeway halted the whiskey glass halfway to his lips. "Why? The others got cash."

"I don't have enough cash," Travis said frankly. "Army script is the same as gold. Mr. Janeway, I don't really see how you can object."

"Well, of all the damned crust! Before you stuck your nose in I got Dodge City prices for my cattle—"

"Which was unfair."

"—All right, all right! But then when a man takes pity on some thirsty steers and lets them drink a little too much water—"

"He shouldn't complain when he gets caught," Travis finished for him.

Janeway tossed off the whiskey and banged the glass on the desk. "Now you want me to take script when the homesteaders get cash. Let's see you make that right."

"You must have *some* cash," Travis said. "These homesteaders have none. And they need it to improve their lot. Janeway, somewhere along the line, you've gotten the idea that the ills of your fellow men are of no expense to you. You've got to put yourself out a little to help them. If you put as much thought into reaching a hand down to help some other man off his knees as you did figuring out a way to get paid for a few extra pounds per steer that crossed my scale, you'd be quite an asset to this country."

With a rush Janeway came to his feet, his fists clenched, and Major Deacon used a tone heretofore reserved for dressing down impudent young officers. "Sit down!" Janeway whipped his head about and stared at Deacon, who speared him with his eyes. "Mr. Janeway, I rarely repeat myself."

Slowly, Janeway eased himself back into his chair. Deacon kept watching him. Then he said, "Mr. Janeway, in my book, Mr. Travis is the best thing that's happened since Sheridan's march to the sea. You are fortunate that I'm not sitting behind that desk, for if I had been, I would have had you thrown off the reservation!" He let his voice rise until it was a shout when he reached the end of the sentence. He went on in a calmer voice. "Once, when I was a young second lieutenant, I shared Mr. Travis' tolerant views, and I also strained my God-given understanding trying to put up with men like you. My patience is now frayed a little thin, and in ten years Mr. Travis will find himself the

165

same way. I suppose that's why we need the very young, Mr. Janeway; they will tolerate such nonsense from men like you, who should know better."

Janeway kept rolling the brim of his hat in his hands, then he got up and went outside and walked across to the holding pens for his horse.

"I suppose I should have kept my mouth shut," Deacon said. "But that damned man needed telling off, Mr. Travis." He sighed and searched his pockets for a cigar, and found one. "In the future I'll keep my nose out of your business."

"I'm grateful for the major's support," Travis said sincerely.

Deacon extended his hand. "My name's Ralph. Formality seems a little misplaced, since we're both in the same army." He slapped his lean stomach. "Who does the cooking around here? And is it fit to eat?"

Dodge City lay three days to the north, and they left Friday evening in the ambulance, Sergeant Slattery, the major's personal orderly, in command of the four-man escort.

Busik was placed in charge of the reservation, and since Arness' fever had broken and only time was needed to put him on his feet, Summers returned to Spanish Spring on horseback.

During his journey to Fort Winthrop, Jefferson Travis had stayed over five days at Fort Dodge and met the town first-hand, but that was hardly long enough to make acquaintances at the garrison, let alone friends. And this time, when the officer of the day showed them their quarters, the atmosphere was decidedly chilly.

Major Deacon was billeted with the staff officers while Travis was given a small room in the bachelor officers' row. He dined at a table with four others, but he might as well have been eating alone, for they cleverly blocked him from their conversation.

At eight o'clock an orderly summoned him to Quarters A, and he found Major Deacon on the porch.

"We only have time for a word," Deacon said, "which is why I waited here. Now we find out what the rules are going to be."

They went inside and were taken by an orderly to the colonel's drawing room. He was a tall, robust man, fifty-some, with a distinguished career behind him. A lieutenant introduced them.

"Colonel Keene, Lieutenant-Colonel Farnsworth, and Major Griswald. Would you all be seated, gentlemen?"

Major Griswald nodded coldly to Travis, and smiled a little "I told you so" with his eyes. Colonel Keene was a bearded man, the commanding officer in the general's absence, while Lt. Col. Farnsworth acted as executive officer. He was older than Keene, rather thin and wan in complexion, and his military career had been not only difficult, but rather uneventful.

"Gentlemen," Keene said in a very soft voice, "I thought it would be best if we all sat down and had a talk before the proceedings begin tomorrow morning. First, since the case is going to be tried here, Colonel Farnsworth has agreed to handle the prosecution."

"I understood that I was to handle that, sir," Deacon said bluntly.

"Quite so, but the general—who regrets his absence—thought Colonel Farnsworth more suited." He frowned slightly.

"But sir," Deacon protested, "I'm fully familiar with the case. As you know, I was on the spot."

"Precisely, Major." Colonel Keene was patient. "We

want no hint of partisanship in this case. In any case, I hardly think it's worth making an issue over."

"Very well," Deacon said resignedly. "I assume, sir, that the charges remain unchanged."

"Yes, generally speaking," Keene said. "Major Griswald, who is acting legal officer, gave the whole matter his studied attention, and felt that a conviction would be more certain if we disregarded the actual killing of Swain, and based our case on the girl's attack."

"Why?" Jefferson asked.

They looked at him in much the way parents do when they believe children should be seen and not heard. Colonel Keene said, "Lieutenant, what difference does it make what a man is hanged for?"

"Two charges, sir, enhance the possibility of his hanging," Travis said.

"Well, we don't wish to debate the matter, Mr. Travis," Griswald said coolly. "I believe our judgment in this case is sound."

"I trust, major, that it's more sound than your auditing of Regan's books."

Griswald surged erect, his face livid, and Keene held up his hands. "Now, we're not going to argue. Mr. Travis, that remark was highly out of order! I want to hear no more of it!" His glance touched Major Ralph Deacon. "I'll expect, sir, that some measure of reprimand be taken against Mr. Travis for his impertinence."

"Impertinence, sir?" Deacon was a picture of innocence. "I was assuming that Mr. Travis made a conjecture based on fact. I have, sirs, his report, as yet unforwarded, concerning certain discrepancies in the auditing of Regan's books. And it was my

168

understanding that the trading post was going to be reopened. Yet when I used the crossing the place was still padlocked."

"There has been a change in policy," Farnsworth said, in his reedy voice. "We've canceled Regan's trading permit and have no intention of reopening the post." He glanced at Colonel Keene. "Must we discuss the matter any further?"

"I think it will bear a great deal of discussion," Deacon said firmly, prodding the point. "Can it be, gentlemen, that there's been some sleight of hand between Regan and Major Griswald that has been settled in the privacy of the immediate family?"

"*You're* out of order!" Keene snapped. "Don't mince words with me, major! By God, I won't put up with it!" He turned his wrath on Jefferson Travis: "Haven't you stirred up enough?"

"Yes, sir, I suppose so. But the colonel must admit that I can't be blamed for the twister."

Deacon laughed aloud, for he had been jolted by this blunt honesty at their first meeting, and it was amusing to see the shocked surprise on Colonel Keene's face. Griswald came to his feet, shouting, and Keene pounded his fist on the table to restore order.

"Gentlemen, we are accomplishing nothing," he said. "Can't we agree on the charges?"

"Yes, sir," Travis said. "Murder and rape, sir."

Keene's frown was a thundercloud. "Mr. Travis, you are a witness, and that is all. We're setting the charges, whether you approve of them or not. You will hold yourself in readiness on the post until the time you are called." He looked at Major Deacon. "Now you go ahead and forward any report you want, and I'll kill it before it ever reaches the general's desk. Is that clear?

169

Colonel Farnsworth and Major Griswald have prepared their case carefully, and they're going to present it. I think that will be all, gentlemen."

When they were outside, Deacon said, "I hope you noticed how rank was pulled, Jeff."

"Pulled? I thought we were being smothered by it." He bit off the end of a cigar and put a match to it. "You hit pretty close to home concerning Griswald. He was probably taking a bit for his own pocket, and in turn letting Regan have a little more rope to swing."

"Well, it happens in the best of armies," Deacon said. "Can't blame them for wanting it hushed up. I've hushed up a few myself." He hesitated, as though considering a point. "I don't understand why they want to charge Clayman with rape and not murder. To me it weakens the whole case."

"How can they drop one? The charges are specific."

"By presenting all admissible evidence in one direction and not much in the other." He looked through his own pockets for a cigar, then took one offered by Travis. "I'd like to know for certain whether or not Keene really wants a conviction. He covered up for Griswald—" He let the rest trail off. "Well, we'll know more in the morning when the trial opens."

Travis spent the rest of the evening writing letters to his family, and it was a chore because he couldn't keep his mind on his writing. Yet he managed to fill several pages and put them in an envelope, then took it to the officer of the day, who would see that it got on the eastbound train.

He slept poorly, and in the morning dabbled listlessly at his breakfast, then went to his room to put on his parade uniform, supplied by the Fort Dodge quartermaster for the occasion.

The trial was being held in the headquarters building, and the parade ground was crowded with buffalo hunters. As Travis pushed his way through and gained the porch, Luke Spears turned from a group of men and stared at him. Spears was shaved and wore a tight-fitting suit. A derby was perched on one side of his head, and he came over to Travis, smiling without warmth.

"Well, if it ain't the little soldier boy. Say, I heard you had a little fun on the prairie not long ago. I sure hope you buried Swilling deep. He always had a fear of dying out there and being ate by varmints." He reached out and poked Travis on the chest. "You going to testify against poor Clayman? Well, you go right ahead, and when you're through, I'll be in Dodge waiting for you."

"Don't waste your time," Travis said coolly.

"I don't look at it that way," Spears said. "I just add up the cost of six wagons loaded with green hides, and the wages I paid out, which are all gone now, and shooting you becomes real pleasurable. If you don't come into town, I'll likely meet you somewhere on the way home. And I won't bother to bury *you*."

He wheeled then and went back to his friends, and Travis went on inside to sit in the hallway until he was called. At nine o'clock, the prosecutor, Colonel Farnsworth, made his charge to the court, but this took place behind closed doors and Travis heard none of it. Then a side door opened and a junior officer came in with the Swain girl. Travis was at first surprised to see her, then he reasoned it out quickly: Colonel Keene had sent an officer to Spanish Spring for her, and to make sure it was done quietly, he had taken the stage both ways. Very clever of the prosecution, Travis admitted to himself, and then wondered how deeply this cleverness extended.

He was not called until the middle of the afternoon. The Swain girl had already corroborated the charges to the satisfaction of the court.

This was a closed hearing, with only the court and the accused present. The room was small and drab, and the shades were drawn. He was sworn in and took the stand to the left of the judge.

Lt. Col. Farnsworth asked all the questions: they were simple enough, dealing with every phase of the girl's recovery, and the subsequent arrest of Clayman. The two depositions had already been introduced as evidence. Travis had an opportunity to see Clayman's legal counsel, two distinguished civilians who more than likely had a formidable reputation for acquittals, and he wondered who was footing the bill for them. Clayman's buffalo hunting friends, or someone with high military rank, who had an alliance with the big moneyed hide buyers? He supposed he never would know.

Farnsworth was very good with questions; all of them could be answered yes or no. And the defense counsels were very quick on their feet every time Travis tried to volunteer a statement. They lost no time in having it stricken from the records as voluntary. So he ended up sketching in what Farnsworth wanted sketched in, and he never got to tell them about Swain dying in the storeroom with a buffalo-rifle bullet clear through him.

That night, Major Deacon came around and they sat until quite late, talking it over, trying to decide how it was going to come out. The prosecution was resting its case on the statements of two people, Travis, and the Swain girl, who could only answer by nodding her head.

Neither Deacon nor Jefferson Travis liked this, but they couldn't do anything about it, not and continue to pursue a military career.

The next day, when he returned for cross-examination by the defense lawyers, it seemed that one did all the talking while the other did all the thinking, for after a few questions, Mr. Skyler, who talked, always went back to the defense table to listen to Mr. Lavery.

"Mr. Travis," Skyler said, approaching the witness. "You're an ambitious young man, aren't you?"

"Leading the witness," Farnsworth said, as though he didn't really care.

"Rephrase your question," the judge said.

"Are you an ambitious young man?" Skyler repeated.

Travis wondered how a man answered such a question. By saying no and having the army put it on record, or saying yes and opening himself for a low punch?

"I suppose I am," he said.

"Did you see the accused attack the Swain girl, Mr. Travis?"

"No, sir."

"I see." He went back for another conference and brought back the two depositions. "Do you recognize these? The prosecution has entered them as evidence."

"Yes, I recognize them."

"This deposition, signed by an X, how was it obtained?" He regarded Travis with some amusement. "Voluntarily, or by threat?"

"They are signed," Travis said. "And witnessed."

"I quite understand that," Mr. Skyler said. "And I understand a great deal more, Mr. Travis. Isn't it true that you rode into the buffalo camp and demanded to search it?"

"I told Spears I *wanted* to search it."

"Ah, yes, that was it. You considered it your right to

173

invade their privacy?"

"We were searching for those left homeless or injured by the twister, and it was suggested to me that I examine Spears' camp. To answer your question, I considered it a duty to search it."

"And when Mr. Spears objected, you threw him to the ground; isn't that correct?"

"I was defending myself. He reached for his pistol."

Mr. Lavery hissed and Skyler went to the table for a whispered conference. Skyler came back. "Mr. Travis, we'll skip all that. Isn't it true, that in order to ascertain the identity of the defendant, who is accused of molesting the Swain girl, you threatened to hang another man?"

"Yes," Travis said. "But why do you insist on calling it molesting when the charge is—"

"Just answer the questions," Skyler interrupted sharply. "And at the reservation, Mr. Travis, isn't it true that you threatened to turn Mr. Spears out on the prairie afoot and unarmed, unless he confessed?"

"Yes, but you don't bluff a man like Spears."

"Your Honor, can we have that last stricken?"

"Strike it out." He looked at Travis. "Just answer the questions."

Skyler said, "Mr. Travis, wasn't the other man beaten and threatened also?"

"Not beaten in relation to his deposition."

"Threatened then?"

"I used harsh words with him," Travis admitted. "You don't get anywhere with a man like that by—"

"Your Honor—?" Skyler said.

"Strike it out," the judge said. "Mr. Travis, please just answer the questions."

"He's twisting my words and meaning to suit his

174

case!" Travis said indignantly.

"I'm through with the witness," Skyler said smoothly, returning to his chair.

"You may step down." the judge said.

"But that's not all there is to it," Travis protested. He looked at Farnsworth, who was paring his fingernails with a pocket knife. Anger made his cheeks stiff, and he stepped down and walked from the room, his heels trouncing the floor.

In the hallway, where he met Major Deacon, he found himself still too angry to speak, and he went outside to stand, trying to cool off.

13

NEITHER MAJOR RALPH DEACON NOR JEFFERSON
Travis expected the trial to last more than two days, and
when it went into the fifth, they expressed a common
worry, for the defense was making a strong bid to
discredit Travis and the depositions.

Unable to attend the trial as a spectator, Travis picked
up information through Deacon, who had enough rank
to find out what was going on. With the prosecution
resting on the testimony of Travis and the Swain girl,
and backed only by the two depositions, the defense
attorneys had a free hand in kicking the supports out
from under it all.

They drew their witnesses from the buffalo hunters,
several of whom swore that they had been on familiar
terms with the Swain girl from time to time, and even
went so far as to maintain that they had her father's
blessing, since they always paid, cash in hand. The
buffalo hunters made a good impression on the court
with their behavior and dress; they all wore dark suits
and ties and spoke softly without swearing, and every
lie became the truth.

Spears was put on the stand, and no amount of cross-
examination by Lt. Col. Farnsworth could shake his
testimony; he was a man set upon by an impetuous
young officer and an irresponsible army. Clayman was
innocent, for the girl went along of her own free will,
and when Clayman took the stand to tell his story, it was
of a life well intentioned, but misspent. He claimed to
have been an orphan with little religious upbringing,
and his only crime was to take the girl to his blankets

176

without benefit of clergy. It was true that her father had been shot, but only in self-defense. They had argued over price and Swain had lost his temper.

It took half a day for the defense to sum up, and forty minutes for the prosecution. The court then adjourned until ten the next morning, when the judge would announce the verdict. That night Travis ate his supper in Major Deacon's quarters, and they talked.

Jefferson Travis had some outspoken opinions: "Colonel Farnsworth just threw away the charges, major. The man is either a fool or he's making sure Clayman is acquitted."

"It wouldn't be the first time the army whitewashed anyone," Deacon reminded him. "You must have been in grade school when Colonel Chivington perpetrated the Sand Creek Massacre. A lot of people wanted him drawn and quartered for that, but the army fooled around and slapped his wrists and turned him scot-free. A few years later, Colonel Carrington went through his brief and tragic fiasco at Fort Kearney. He was recalled, of course, but he was never court-martialed for his part in the gross mismanagement of the campaign." He sighed and opened his cigar case. "Jeff, the army wants this over and a right decision rendered. You were the principal witness and you weren't on the stand an hour. It's obvious that you were only supposed to give token testimony."

"Something ought to be done about it!"

"Nothing can be done about it," Deacon said flatly. "And you know it."

"Yes, but that doesn't make it any easier to take." He accepted one of Deacon's cigars, and a light. "That poor Swain girl, unable to answer the lies told about her."

"In the old days they used to have the sacrificial

lamb," Deacon said. "But in the army we use anyone who's handy. Including second lieutenants." He leaned forward and added, "Jeff, be thankful they didn't ruin your career. But bear in mind, they would have if there hadn't been any other way."

"Major, Clayman will be acquitted, won't he?"

Deacon hesitated a moment before answering. "Yes. It's in the cards. I suppose I knew all along how it would be, how it had to be. But I don't want you to turn bitter over it, Jeff. I don't want you to think everything you did was for nothing."

"Well, wasn't it, sir? Can you honestly say that it wasn't?" He let his anger out; it put strength into his voice.

"Nothing we do, good or bad, is totally for nothing," Deacon said. "If I knew whether you were really army, I'd know you understood that. It's a slow, tedious game we play at, Jeff, and sometimes, measuring it by the span of a man's service life, it doesn't seem like we accomplish very much, but we really do. You put it all together and we do."

"If the next forty years are going to be like this, sir, I don't want to think about them."

Deacon studied him carefully. "Thinking of resigning, Jeff?"

The young man shrugged. "Right now, sir, I feel like poking some staff officer in the nose." He drew on his cigar until he was calm again. "I suppose that's not very 'army,' sir, to want to poke a colonel in the nose."

"We don't do it in the army," Deacon said softly. "There's no mark on your record, Jeff. Why don't you be glad of that; it gives you a chance to go on, to try again."

"Is it worth it, sir?" He shook his head. "Right now I

don't think it is."

Someone knocked on the front door and the orderly, who was in the kitchen washing the supper dishes, went to answer it. He came into the parlor a moment later and said, "It's Major Griswald, sir. He offers his compliments and—"

"Invite the major in," Deacon said, and got up to have a drink ready.

Griswald came in, his heels clicking smartly on the bare floor. He sailed his hat onto a corner chair, and took the drink in his left hand so he could unfasten his collar.

"Well, the beastly affair is over," he said. "My, that's good whiskey." He glanced at Travis briefly. "Cheer up, Mr. Travis. There will be other days in court."

"Will there, sir?"

Griswald laughed. "You have to learn how to ride with the punches, Travis. Isn't that right, major?"

"It helps to minimize the bruises," Deacon admitted. "How is the verdict going to go, Griswald?"

"Guilty," he said, then sat down and crossed his legs. "A telegram arrived last night from the general; the whole complexion's changed." He looked at Travis. "You look surprised. Don't be. The buffalo are being killed off rapidly. In three more years there won't be any hunters on the prairie. There's no sense coddling a dead horse, Travis. Makes sense, doesn't it?"

"So you're going to hang Clayman because it's no longer profitable to let him go," Travis said. "I don't like the reason."

Griswald finished his drink. "Travis, we're hanging him because he's guilty. Justice has been served and you're Queen of the May." He got up and flourished his hand. "You've done a good job, Mr. Travis. Damn it,

179

though, for a while, there I thought you were going to put salt on my tail, but all you ended up with was some feathers."

"I may get a little meat the next time," Travis said frankly.

"Then I'll have to watch myself." Griswald said. "And I'll be watching your career closely, so see that you make no mistakes." He looked at Deacon, who was sitting there, glancing from one to the other, and staying clear of this. "Travis, my boy, if we didn't keep our eye on one another, we'd all be thieves. The easy way out is always there, and generally we'll take it because doing right is often one hell of a lot of trouble. For myself, I'm glad Clayman is going to be hung; the buffalo hunters have been out of hand for some time." He reached over and put his glass on the table. "Well, I must be going. Colonel Keene's giving a small, private party, to celebrate, I suppose. In the morning he'll send the general a wire, relaying the verdict, and then he can forsake his Arkansas mud baths and come back; the smoke will have cleared by then." He got up and buttoned his blouse and put on his hat. Then he walked over to Travis and offered his hand. The young man stared at it for a moment, then accepted it and Major Griswald laughed. "Happy hunting, Mr. Travis. I'm sure we'll both enjoy it immensely." Then he winked broadly. "And if Deacon proves too much of a bastard for you, transfer into my command. I can always use an able officer."

He went out then, as briskly as he had come in, and when the front door slammed shut, Jefferson Travis wiped a hand across his mouth and stared at Major Ralph Deacon.

"Well, Jeff, why didn't you poke him in the nose?"

"It's nothing but a damned game," Travis said softly. "I thought I'd made an enemy in Major Griswald, but it isn't so at all. He'd tear me limb from limb if he had to, or thought it would suit some purpose, but there wouldn't be anything personal in it. Would there?"

"No," Deacon said. "Why didn't you hit him?"

Jefferson Travis shook his head. "I don't know. Do you?"

"Yes," he said. "I know. Because you're 'army,' Jeff. Like it or not, you're a career soldier, in until sixty-five, retirement age. You'll cuss and fume and swear you'll get out, but you're army and there isn't anything you can do about it, because you're made to soldier. Griswald knew it, sensed it; most career soldiers can sooner or later. Myself? I wasn't sure. Not until you sat there and listened to him without flying off the handle." He got up and poured two drinks, handing one to Jefferson Travis. "Are you going to stick around and watch Clayman hang?"

"No, I guess not, sir."

"What are your plans?"

Travis thought for a moment, then shrugged. "Go back to Spanish Spring and start all over again, I suppose. And hope for better luck next time."

"Maybe you'll get it," Deacon said. "You've brought a few problems to your door though. Spears is going to be looking for you and the buffalo hunters are going to blame you for Clayman's hanging."

Travis drank some of the whiskey and enjoyed the fire in his stomach. "Spears doesn't really scare me much, sir. If he wants a fight, I'll accommodate him." He looked at Deacon, "The reservation's a mess; I'll have to straighten that out as soon as I get back or the Indians will leave." He sighed. "That will be a thankless

181

job, I can tell you. And there isn't any real peace around Spanish Spring. I'll have to do something about that before I get much older." He raised his glass until he could see the bottom, then set it aside and leaned back. "Major, what the hell am I going to do with Ben Arness? He and I never hit it off on the right foot, and he even made up his mind that he wanted to leave the army. It's really my fault because I've ridden him too hard."

Ralph Deacon laughed. "Jeff, I've know Arness for twenty years and he's threatened to leave the army periodically. But he can't leave. He's a soldier, and he's stuck, the same as we are. Sure, he hates young lieutenants; he hated me once, but young lieutenants sometimes get to be old captains. Give him another year or so, Jeff. He'll come around. He always has." Deacon chuckled. "He'll marry that Beaumont woman and she'll take some of the starch out of him."

"I expect I'll take a horse back," Travis said, rising. He seemed eager to leave, as though his duties were pressing and he just had to get at them. "I'm going to work on General Thomas C. Wrigley and see if I can't break his stranglehold on the homesteaders. Of course, it'll pay to keep an eye on those cattlemen too; they're a rough lot, bent on having their own way." He stopped talking and turned his head as someone knocked. The orderly answered the door.

He came to the parlor and said, "A Mr. Jamison to see Mr. Travis, sir."

"Show him in," Deacon said.

Eldredge Jamison was a man in his young thirties, very well dressed, and he carried a malacca cane with an ebony head. A celluloid collar forced him to keep his head high, and he swept off his beaver, holding it in the

182

crook of his left arm.

"Have I the pleasure of addressing Lieutenant Jefferson Travis, commanding the Spanish Spring detachment?"

"I'm Travis." He neither smiled nor frowned. "How can I be of service?"

"By hearing me, sir, and I shall be brief," Jamison said crisply, his voice full of the brittleness of New England. "I wish to inform you, sir, that I have been appointed Indian agent to succeed the late Mr. Brewer. I've had experience before with the army, and I want it clearly understood that I'll brook no interference whatsoever: The Indians are under the jurisdiction of the Interior Department, while you represent the War Department; the name alone implies its purpose. If I need you, I'll summon you. In any other event, do not disturb the Indians, as I intend to instill in them Christian habits and various agricultural pursuits." He bowed to Major Deacon. "I've disturbed you. I'm sorry. Good night."

They stared at the door after it slammed shut, then Travis laughed, a soft rumble in his throat. He did this twice, then a gale of laughter poured from him and he and Deacon slapped each other on the back and held each other up, laughing until tears ran down their cheeks.

Finally they checked their mirth and Deacon picked up the bottle of whiskey and empty glasses. "You want to kill this for the road, Jeff?"

"Pour," Travis said, and sat down, feeling strong and mature and completely at ease, completely satisfied with himself and his lot.

Wade Everett, a pseudonym for Will Cook, is the author of numerous outstanding Western novels as well as historical frontier fiction. He was born in Richmond, Indiana, but was raised by an aunt and uncle in Cambridge, Illinois. He joined the U.S. cavalry at the age of sixteen but was disillusioned because horses were being eliminated through mechanization. He transferred to the U.S. Army Air Force in which he served in the South Pacific during the Second World War. Cook turned to writing in 1951 and contributed a number of outstanding short stories to *Dime Western* and other pulp magazines as well as fiction for major smooth-paper magazines such as *The Saturday Evening Post.* It was in the *Post* that his best-known novel, *Comanche Captives,* was serialized. It was later filmed as *Two Rode Together* (Columbia, 1961) directed by John Ford and starring James Stewart and Richard Widmark. It has now been restored, as was the author's intention, with *The Peacemakers* set in 1870 as the first part and *Comanche Captives* set in 1874 as the second part of a major historical novel titled *Two Rode Together.* Sometimes in his short stories Cook would introduce characters that would later be featured in novels, such as Charlie Boomhauer who first appeared in *Lawmen Die Sudden* in *Big-Book Western* in 1953 and is later to be found in *Badman's Holiday* (1958) and *The Wind River Kid* (1958). Along with his steady productivity, Cook maintained an enviable quality. His novels range widely in time and place, from the Illinois frontier of 1811 to southwest Texas in 1905, but each is peopled with credible and interesting characters whose interactions form the backbone of the narrative. Most of his novels deal with more or less traditional Western themes— range wars, reformed outlaws, cattle rustling, Indian

184

fighting—but there are also romantic novels such as *Sabrina Kane* (1956) and exercises in historical realism such as *Elizabeth, by Name* (1958). Indeed, his fiction is known for its strong heroines. Another common feature is Cook's compassion for his characters who must be able to survive in a wild and violent land. His protagonists make mistakes, hurt people they care for, and sometimes succumb to ignoble impulses, but this all provides an added dimension to the artistry of his work.

We hope that you enjoyed reading this
Sagebrush Large Print Western.
If you would like to read more Sagebrush titles,
ask your librarian or contact the Publishers:

United States and Canada

Thomas T. Beeler, *Publisher*
Post Office Box 659
Hampton Falls, New Hampshire 03844-0659
(800) 818-7574

United Kingdom, Eire, and the Republic of South Africa

Isis Publishing Ltd
7 Centremead
Osney Mead
Oxford OX2 0ES England
(01865) 250333

Australia and New Zealand

Bolinda Publishing Pty. Ltd.
17 Mohr Street
Tullamarine, 3043, Victoria, Australia
(016103) 9338 0666